ONCE HUNTED

(A RILEY PAIGE MYSTERY—BOOK 5)

BLAKE PIERCE

ISBN: 978-1-63291-858-1

BOOKS BY BLAKE PIERCE

RILEY PAIGE MYSTERY SERIES
ONCE GONE (Book #1)
ONCE TAKEN (Book #2)
ONCE CRAVED (Book #3)
ONCE LURED (Book #4)
ONCE HUNTED (Book #5)
ONCE PINED (Book #6)

MACKENZIE WHITE MYSTERY SERIES
BEFORE HE KILLS (Book #1)
BEFORE HE SEES (Book #2)
BEFORE HE COVETS (Book #3)

AVERY BLACK MYSTERY SERIES
CAUSE TO KILL (Book #1)
CAUSE TO RUN (Book #2)

PROLOGUE

Special Agent Riley Paige's speeding car shattered the silence of Fredericksburg's dark streets. Her fifteen-year-old daughter was missing, but Riley was more furious than frightened. She had a good idea where April was—with her new boyfriend, seventeen-year-old high school dropout Joel Lambert. Riley had tried her best to put a stop to the relationship, but she hadn't been successful.

Tonight that's going to change, she thought with determination.

She parked in front of Joel's home, a rundown little house in an unsavory neighborhood. She'd been here once before and had given Joel an ultimatum to stay away from her daughter. He'd obviously ignored it.

There wasn't a single light on in the house. Maybe nobody was even inside. Or maybe what Riley would find in there would be more than she could handle. She didn't care. She banged on the door.

"Joel Lambert! Open up!" she yelled.

There were a few moments of silence. Riley banged on the door again. This time she heard muttered curses inside. The porch light came on. Still chained, the door opened a few inches. In the light from the porch, Riley could make out an unfamiliar face. It was a bearded, strung-out-looking man of about nineteen or twenty.

"What do you want?" the man asked groggily.

"I'm here for my daughter," Riley said.

The man looked puzzled.

"You've got the wrong place, lady," he said.

He tried to shut the door, but Riley kicked it so hard that the safety chain broke loose and the door flew open.

"Hey!" the man yelled.

Riley stormed inside. The house looked much as it had the last time she'd been here—a horrible mess filled with suspicious odors. The young man was tall and wiry. Riley detected a family resemblance between him and Joel. But he wasn't old enough to be Joel's father.

"Who are you?" she asked.

"I'm Guy Lambert," he replied.

"Joel's brother?" Riley guessed.

"Yeah. Who the hell are you?"

Riley whipped out her badge.

"Special Agent Riley Paige, FBI," she said.

The man's eyes got wide with alarm.

"FBI? Hey, there's got to be some kind of mistake here."

"Are your parents here?" Riley said.

Guy Lambert shrugged.

"Parents? What parents? Joel and I are on our own here."

Riley was hardly surprised. The last time she'd been here, she'd suspected that Joel's parents were out of the picture. What had become of them she couldn't possibly guess.

"Where's my daughter?" Riley said.

"Lady, I don't even know your daughter."

Riley took a step toward the nearest doorway. Guy Lambert tried to block her way.

"Hey, aren't you supposed to have a search warrant?" he asked.

Riley thrust him aside.

"I'm making the rules right now," she snarled.

Riley went through the door into a disheveled bedroom. No one was there. She continued through another door into a filthy bathroom, and another door that connected to a second bedroom. Still no one.

She heard a voice call out from the living room.

"Hold it right there!"

She hurried back into the living room.

Now she saw that her partner, Agent Bill Jeffreys, was standing in the front doorway. She had called for his help before she'd left home. Guy Lambert was slumped on the sofa, looking despondent.

"This guy seemed to be heading out," Bill said. "I just made it clear that he should wait here for you."

"Where are they?" Riley demanded of Lambert. "Where are your brother and my daughter?"

"I've got no idea."

Riley seized him by the T-shirt and hauled him to his feet.

"Where are your brother and my daughter?" she repeated.

When he said, "I don't know," she slammed him against the wall. She heard Bill let out a groan of disapproval. Doubtless he was worried that Riley might get out of control. She didn't care.

Completely panicked now, Guy Lambert spit out an answer.

"They're just down on the next block on this street. Thirteen thirty-four."

Riley released him. Without another word, she stormed out the front door as Bill followed after her.

Riley had her flashlight out and was checking the house numbers. "It's this way," she said.

"We've got to call for some help," Bill said.

"We don't need backup," Riley called as she ran along the sidewalk.

"That's not what worries me." Bill followed her.

In a few moments, Riley stood in the yard of a two-story house. It was broken-down and obviously condemned, with empty lots on either side—a typical "shooting gallery" for heroin users. It reminded her of the house where a sadistic psychopath named Peterson had held her captive. He'd kept her in a cage and tormented her with a propane torch until she'd escaped and blown the place up with his own supply of propane.

For a second, she hesitated, shaken by the memory. But then she reminded herself:

April's in there.

"Get ready," she told Bill.

Bill took out his own flashlight and his gun, and they moved together toward the house.

When Riley arrived at the porch, she saw that the windows were boarded up. She had no intention of knocking this time. She didn't want to give Joel or anyone else who was in there any warning.

She tried the doorknob. It turned. But the door was locked by a deadbolt. She pulled out her gun and fired, blasting the deadbolt away. She turned the knob again and the door fell open.

Even after the darkness outside, her eyes had to adjust as she and Bill stepped into the living room. The only light came from scattered candles. They illuminated a ghastly scene of trash and debris that included empty heroin bags, hypodermics, and other drug paraphernalia. About seven people were visible—two or three of them getting sluggishly to their feet after the racket Riley had made, the rest still lying on the floor or curled up in chairs in a drug-induced stupor. They all looked wasted and ill, and their clothes were filthy and tattered.

Riley holstered her weapon. She clearly didn't need it—not yet.

"Where's April?" she yelled. "Where's Joel Lambert?"

A man who had just stood up said in a foggy voice, "Upstairs."

With Bill behind her, Riley made her way up the dark stairway, shining the flashlight ahead of her. She could feel the rotting steps giving under her weight. She and Bill stepped into the hallway at the top of the stairs. Three doorways, one of them leading into a vile-smelling bathroom, had been stripped of their doors and were visibly empty. The fourth doorway still had a door, and it was shut.

Riley stepped toward the door. Bill held out his hand to stop her.

3

"Let me go in first," he said.

Ignoring him, Riley pushed past him, opened the door, and stepped inside.

Riley's legs almost gave out from under her at what she saw. April was lying on a bare mattress, murmuring "No, no, no" over and over again. She writhed feebly as Joel Lambert struggled to pull off her clothes. An overweight, homely man stood nearby, waiting for Joel to finish his task. A needle and a spoon lay on the candlelit bed stand.

Riley understood in an instant. Joel had drugged April almost into unconsciousness and was offering her as a sexual favor to this repulsive man—whether for money or some other purpose, Riley didn't know.

She drew her weapon again and pointed it at Joel. It was all she could do to restrain herself from shooting him right away.

"Back away from her," she said.

Joel clearly understood her state of mind. He raised his hands and stepped away from the bed.

Indicating the other man, Riley said to Bill, "Cuff this bastard. Take him back to your car. Now you can call for help."

"Riley, listen to me ..." Bill's voice trailed off.

Riley knew what Bill was leaving unsaid. He understood perfectly well that all Riley wanted was a few minutes alone with Joel. He was understandably reluctant to allow that.

Still keeping her gun pointed at Joel, Riley looked at Bill with an imploring expression. Bill slowly nodded, then went over to the man, read him his rights, cuffed him, and led him outside.

Riley shut the door behind them. Then she stood silently facing Joel Lambert, her gun still raised. This was the boy that April had fallen in love with. But this was no ordinary teenager. He was deeply involved with the drug trade. He had used those drugs on her own daughter and had obviously intended to sell April's body. This was not a person capable of loving anyone.

"What do you think you're going to do, cop lady?" he said. "I've got rights, you know." He flashed her the same slightly smirking smile he'd displayed the last time she'd seen him.

The gun trembled slightly in Riley's hand. She was itching to pull the trigger and blow this lowlife away. But she couldn't let herself do that.

She noticed that Joel was edging toward the end table. He was sturdily built, and he was a bit taller than Riley. He was moving toward a baseball bat, obviously kept for self-defense purposes, that

4

was leaning against the table. Riley suppressed a grim smile. It looked like he was going to do exactly what she wanted him to do.

"You're under arrest," she said.

She holstered her weapon and reached for the cuffs on the back of her belt. Exactly as she'd hoped, Joel lunged for the baseball bat, picked it up, and swung it wildly at Riley. She deftly avoided the blow and braced herself for the next swing.

This time Joel raised the bat high, meaning to smash her head with it. But as his arm came down, Riley ducked and reached for the small end of the bat. She grabbed it, then yanked it away from him. She enjoyed the surprised look on his face as he lost his balance.

Joel reached for the end table to stop himself from falling. When his hand was fast against the table, Riley brought the bat crashing down on it. She could hear the bones breaking.

Joel let out a pathetic scream and fell to the floor.

"You crazy bitch!" he yelled. "You broke my hand."

Panting for breath, Riley cuffed him to a bedpost.

"Couldn't help it," she said. "You resisted, and I accidentally slammed your hand in the door. Sorry about that."

Riley cuffed his undamaged hand to the bottom of a bedpost. Then she stepped on his broken hand and shifted her weight onto it.

Joel screamed and writhed. His feet thrashed around helplessly.

"No, no, no!" he shouted.

Still keeping her foot in place, Riley crouched down close to his face.

Mockingly, she said, "'No, no, no!' Where did I hear those words before? Just in the last few minutes?"

Joel was blubbering with pain and terror.

Riley pushed down with her foot.

"Who said it?" she demanded.

"Your daughter … she said it."

"Said what?"

"'No, no, no …'"

Riley let up on the pressure a little.

"And why did my daughter say that?" she asked.

Joel could barely speak through his violent sobs.

"Because … she was helpless … and hurting. I get it. I understand."

Riley removed her foot. She figured he got the message—at least for now, although probably not for good. But this was the best—or worst—she could do for now. He deserved death, or far worse. But she couldn't bring herself to give it to him. At least he would never use that hand properly again.

Riley left Joel, cuffed and cringing, and rushed to her daughter's side. April's eyes were dilated, and Riley knew that she was having trouble seeing her.

"Mom?" April said in a low whimper.

The sound of that word unleashed a world of anguish in Riley. She burst into tears as she started to help April get back into her clothes.

"I'm getting you out of here," she said through her sobs. "Everything's going to be all right."

Yet even as she spoke the words, Riley prayed that they were true.

CHAPTER ONE

Riley was crawling through the dirt in a damp crawlspace under a house. Total darkness surrounded her. She wondered why she hadn't brought a flashlight. After all, she had been in this awful place before.

Again, she heard April's voice call out in the darkness.

"Mom, where are you?"

Despair tugged at Riley's heart. She knew that April was caged somewhere in this evil darkness. She was being tortured by a heartless monster.

"I'm here," Riley called out in reply. "I'm coming. Keep talking so I can find you."

"I'm over here," April called.

Riley crept in that direction, but a moment later she heard her daughter's voice speak from another direction.

"I'm over here."

Then the voice echoed through the darkness.

"I'm over here ... I'm over here ... I'm over here ..."

It wasn't just one voice, and it wasn't just one girl. Many girls were calling for her help. And she had no idea how to reach any of them.

Riley was awakened from her nightmare by a squeeze of her hand. She had fallen asleep holding onto April's hand, and now April was starting to wake up. Riley sat up straighter and looked at her daughter lying in the bed.

April's face was still somewhat pasty and pale, but her hand was stronger and not cold anymore. She looked much better than she had yesterday. Her night in the clinic had done her a lot of good.

April managed to focus her eyes on Riley. Then the tears came, just as Riley knew they would.

"Mom, what if you hadn't come?" April said in a choked voice.

Riley felt her own eyes sting. April had asked the same question countless times now. Riley couldn't bear to even imagine the answer, much less say it aloud.

Riley's cell phone rang. She saw that it was Mike Nevins, a forensic psychiatrist who was also her good friend. He had gotten Riley through a lot of personal crises, and had been glad to help with this one.

"Just checking in," Mike said. "I hope I'm not catching you at a bad time."

Riley was happy to hear Mike's friendly voice.

"Not at all, Mike. Thanks for calling."

"How's she doing?"

"Better, I think."

Riley didn't know what she would have done without Mike's help. After Riley had gotten April away from Joel, yesterday had been a bedlam of emergency services, medical treatments, and police reports. Yesterday evening Mike had arranged for April to be admitted here to the Corcoran Hill Health and Rehab Center.

It was much nicer than the hospital. Even with all the necessary equipment, the room was attractive and comfortable. Through the window Riley could see trees on well-manicured grounds.

Just then, April's doctor came into the room. They ended the call as Dr. Ellis Spears entered, a kindly-looking man with a youthful face but a few telltale gray hairs.

He touched April's hand and asked, "How are you feeling?"

"Not great," she said.

"Well, give yourself some time," he said. "You're going to be fine. Ms. Paige, could I have a word with you?"

Riley nodded and followed him out into the hall. Dr. Spears looked over some information on his clipboard.

"The heroin is almost cleared out of her system now," he said. "The boy gave her a dangerous dose. Fortunately, it leaves the bloodstream quickly. She's not likely to have any more physical withdrawal symptoms. The distress she's going through right now is more emotional than physical."

"Is she going to …?" Riley couldn't bring herself to finish the question.

Fortunately, the doctor understood what she wanted to know.

"Relapse or have cravings? It's hard to say. First-time heroin use can feel wonderful—like nothing else in the world. She's not an addict at this point, but she's not likely to forget that feeling. There's always a danger that she'll be drawn back to the glow it gave her."

Riley grasped what the doctor was getting at. From now on, it was going to be vitally important to keep April away from any possibility of drug use. It was a terrifying prospect. April now admitted to smoking pot and taking pills—some were apparently prescription painkillers, very dangerous opioids.

"Dr. Spears, I—"

For a moment, Riley had trouble forming the question that was on her mind.

"I don't understand what happened," she said. "Why would she do something like this?"

The doctor smiled at her sympathetically. Riley guessed that he heard this question quite often.

"Escape," he said. "But I'm not talking about a complete escape from life. She's not that kind of user. In fact, I don't think she's really a user by nature at all. Like all teenagers, she runs really short on impulse control. That's simply a matter of an immature brain. She really liked the short-term high those drugs gave her. Fortunately, she hasn't used enough to do herself any lasting harm."

Dr. Spears thought silently for a moment.

"Her experience was unusually traumatic," he said. "I'm talking about how that boy was trying to exploit her sexually. That memory alone might be enough to keep her away from drugs for good. But it's also possible that emotional distress could be a dangerous trigger."

Riley's heart sank. Emotional distress seemed an unavoidable fact of family life these days.

"We need to watch her for a few days," Dr. Spears said. "After that, she'll need lots of care, rest, and help with self-analysis."

The doctor excused himself and continued on his rounds. Riley stood in the hall, feeling alone and troubled.

Is this what happened to Jilly? she wondered. *Could April have ended up like that desperate child?*

Two months ago in Phoenix, Arizona, Riley had rescued a girl even younger than April from prostitution. An odd emotional bond had formed between them, and Riley had tried to stay in touch with her after placing her in a shelter for teenagers. But a couple of days ago, Riley had been notified that Jilly had run away. Unable to return to Phoenix, Riley called an FBI agent there for help. She knew the man felt indebted to her, and she expected to hear from him today.

Meanwhile, at least Riley was where she needed to be for April.

She was headed back toward her daughter's room when she heard a voice call her name from down the hallway. She turned and saw the worried face of her ex-husband, Ryan, coming toward her. When she'd called him yesterday to tell him what had happened, he'd been in Minneapolis working on a court case.

Riley was surprised to see him. Ryan's daughter tended to be low on his list of priorities—lower than his job as a lawyer, and much lower than the freedom he was now enjoying as a bachelor. She'd doubted that he would even show up.

9

But now he rushed toward Riley and hugged her, his face full of concern.

"How is she? How is she?"

Ryan kept repeating the question, making it difficult for Riley to reply.

"She's going to be all right," Riley finally managed to say.

Ryan pulled out of the embrace and looked at Riley with an anguished expression.

"I'm sorry," he said. "I'm so, so sorry. You told me that April was having problems, but I didn't listen. I should have been here for both of you."

Riley didn't know what to say. Apologies weren't Ryan's style. In fact, she'd expected him to heap all sorts of blame on her for what had happened. That had always been his normal way of dealing with family crises. Apparently, what had just happened to April was terrible enough to affect him. He had surely already talked with the doctor and learned the whole awful story.

He nodded toward the door.

"Can I see her?" he asked.

"Of course," Riley said.

Riley stood in the doorway and watched as Ryan rushed to April's bed and took her in his arms. He held his daughter tight for a few moments. Riley thought she saw his back heave with a single sob. Then he sat down beside April and held her hand.

April was crying again.

"Oh, Daddy, I messed up so bad," she said. "You see, I was going through this thing with this guy—"

Ryan touched her on the lips to quiet her.

"Shh. You don't need to tell me. It's all right."

Riley felt a lump form in her throat. Suddenly, for the first time in a very long time, she felt as if the three of them were a family. Was that a good thing or a bad thing? Was it a sign of better times to come, or yet another build-up to disappointment and heartbreak? She had no idea.

Riley watched from the doorway as Ryan gently stroked his daughter's hair, and April closed her eyes and relaxed. It was a touching sight.

When did things go so wrong? she wondered.

She found herself wishing she could turn back time to some crucial moment when she'd made some terrible mistake, and do everything differently so that all this would never have happened. She felt pretty sure that Ryan was thinking much the same thing.

It was an ironic thought, and she knew it. The killer she had taken down the day before yesterday had been obsessed with clocks, posing and arranging his victims like hands on a clock face. And now here she was, with her own yearnings about time.

If only I could have kept Peterson away from her, she thought with a shudder.

Like Riley, April had been caged and tormented by that sadistic monster and his propane torch. The poor girl had been struggling with PTSD ever since.

But the truth was, Riley knew that the problem went back further than that.

Maybe if Ryan and I had never gotten divorced, she mused.

But how could that have been avoided? Ryan had been distant and disengaged both as a husband and a father, aside from being a philanderer. Not that she held him solely to blame. She'd made her own share of mistakes. She'd never struck the right balance between her FBI work and being a mother. And she'd not seen a lot of the warning signs that April was headed for trouble.

Her sadness deepened. No, she couldn't think of one particular moment when she could have changed everything. Her life had been too full of mistakes and missed opportunities. Besides, she knew perfectly well that she couldn't turn back time. There was no point in yearning for the impossible.

Her phone rang, and she stepped out into the hallway again. Her heart beat faster when she saw that the call was from Garrett Holbrook, the FBI agent who had taken on the search for Jilly.

"Garrett!" she said, taking the call. "What's going on?"

Garrett answered in his characteristic monotone.

"I've got good news."

Riley immediately started to breathe easier.

"The cops picked her up," Garrett said. "She'd been on the street all night without money or anywhere to go. She got caught shoplifting at a convenience store. I'm with her at the police station right now. I'll post bail, but …"

Garrett stopped. Riley didn't like the sound of that word, "but."

"Maybe I should let her talk to you," he said.

A few seconds later, Riley heard the familiar sound of Jilly's voice.

"Hey, Riley."

Now that Riley's panic was ebbing away, she was starting to get mad.

"Don't 'hey' me. What did you think you were doing, running off like that?"

"I'm not going back there," Jilly said.

"Yes, you are."

"Please don't make me go back there."

Riley didn't reply for a moment. She didn't know what to say. She knew that the shelter where Jilly had been staying was a good, nurturing place. Riley had gotten to know some of the staff, who had been very helpful.

But Riley also understood how Jilly felt. The last time they'd talked together, Jilly had complained that nobody wanted her, that foster parents kept passing her over.

"They don't like my past," Jilly had said.

That conversation had ended badly, with Jilly in tears begging for Riley to adopt her. Riley had been unable to explain the thousand reasons why that was impossible. She hoped this conversation wasn't going to end the same way.

Before Riley could think of what to say, Jilly said, "Your friend wants to talk to you."

Riley heard Garrett Holbrook's voice again.

"She keeps saying that—she won't go back to the shelter. But I've got an idea. One of my sisters, Bonnie, is thinking of adopting. I'm sure that she and her husband would love to have Jilly. That is, if Jilly—"

He was interrupted by squeals of delight from Jilly, who kept yelling, "Yes, yes, yes!" over and over again.

Riley smiled. It was just the kind of moment she needed right now.

"Sounds like a plan, Garrett," she said. "Let me know how it works out. Thanks so much for all your help."

"Any time," Garrett said.

They ended the phone call. Riley stepped back into the doorway and saw that Ryan and April were now carrying on what seemed to be a carefree conversation. Things suddenly seemed so much better. For all of her failings, and Ryan's too, they'd given April a much better life than many other kids had.

Just then she felt a hand on her shoulder and heard a voice.

"Riley."

She turned and saw Bill's friendly face. As she stepped away from the doorway to talk with him, Riley couldn't help glancing back and forth from her longtime partner to her ex-husband. Even in his current state of distress, Ryan looked like the successful lawyer that he was. His blond good looks and smooth manners opened doors for him everywhere. Bill, as she had often realized, looked more like she did. His dark hair showed touches of gray and he was more solid and much more rumpled than Ryan. But Bill was competent in his own areas of expertise and he had been much more dependable in her life.

"How's she doing?" Bill asked.

"Better. What's going on with Joel Lambert?"

Bill shook his head.

"That little thug really is a piece of work," he said. "He's talking, anyway. He says he knows some guys who made a lot of money off of young girls, and he thought he'd give it a try himself. No signs of remorse, he's a sociopath to the bone. Anyway, he'll definitely be convicted and get jail time. He'll probably do a plea deal, though."

Riley frowned. She hated plea deals. And this one was especially upsetting.

"I know how you feel about that," Bill said. "But my guess is he'll talk up a storm, and we'll be able to put a lot of bastards away. That's a good thing."

Riley nodded. It helped to know that some good was going to come out of this terrible ordeal. But there was something she needed to talk about with Bill, and she wasn't sure how to say it.

"Bill, about my coming back to work …"

Bill patted her on the shoulder.

"You don't have to tell me," he said. "You can't work cases for a while. You need to take some time off. Don't worry, I understand. So will everybody at Quantico. Take as much time as you need."

He looked at his watch.

"I'm sorry to rush off, but—"

"Go," Riley said. "And thanks for everything."

She hugged Bill, and he left. Riley stood in the hallway, thinking about the near future.

"Take as much time as you need," Bill had said.

That might not be easy. What had just happened to April was a reminder of all the evil that was out there. It was her job to stop as much of it as she could. And if she'd learned one thing in life, it was that the evil never rested.

CHAPTER TWO

Seven weeks later

When Riley arrived at the psychologist's office, she found Ryan sitting alone in the waiting room.

"Where's April?" she asked.

Ryan nodded toward a closed door.

"She's with Dr. Sloat," he said, sounding uneasy. "They had something they needed to talk about alone. Then we're supposed to go in and join them."

Riley sighed and sat down in a nearby chair. She, Ryan, and April had spent many emotionally demanding hours here during recent weeks. This would be their last session with the psychologist before they all took a break for the Christmas holidays.

Dr. Sloat had insisted that the whole family participate in April's recovery. It had been hard work for all of them. But to Riley's relief, Ryan had taken part wholeheartedly in the process. He'd come to all the sessions that he could fit into his schedule, and he'd even scaled back his work to make more time for this. Today he'd driven April here from her school.

Riley studied her ex-husband's face as he stared at the office door. In many ways, he seemed like a changed man. Not long ago, he'd been inattentive to the point of serious delinquency as a parent. He'd always insisted that all of April's problems were Riley's fault.

But April's drug use and her much-too-close brush with forced prostitution had changed something in Ryan. After her stay in the rehab clinic, April had been home with Riley for six weeks now. Ryan had visited often and had joined them for Thanksgiving. At times, they seemed almost like a functional family.

But Riley kept reminding herself that they had never really been a functional family.

Could that change now? she wondered. *Do I want it to change?*

Riley felt torn, even a little guilty. She'd long tried to accept that her own future probably didn't have Ryan in it. Perhaps there might even be another man in her life.

There had always been some kind of attraction between her and Bill. But they'd also fought and quarreled from time to time. Besides, their professional relationship was demanding enough without throwing romance into the mix.

Her kind and attractive next door neighbor, Blaine, seemed a better prospect, especially since his daughter, Crystal, was April's best friend.

Still, at times like now, Ryan almost seemed to be the same man she'd fallen in love with so many years ago. Where were things headed? She really didn't know.

The office door opened and Dr. Lesley Sloat stepped out.

"We'd like to see you now," she said with a smile.

Riley had long since taken a liking to the short, stocky, good-natured psychologist, and April was clearly fond of her too.

Riley and Ryan both went into the office and sat down in a couple of comfortable upholstered chairs. They were facing April, who sat on a couch beside Dr. Sloat. April was smiling weakly. Dr. Sloat nodded for her to start talking.

"Something happened this week," April said. "It's kind of hard to talk about …"

Riley's breathing quickened and she felt her heart beating faster.

"It's got to do with Gabriela," April said. "Maybe she should be here today to talk about this too, but she's not, so …"

April's voice trailed off.

Riley was surprised. Gabriela was a stout, middle-aged Guatemalan woman who had been the family's housekeeper for years. She had moved in with Riley and April and was like a member of the family.

April took a deep breath and continued, "A couple of days ago, she told me something I didn't tell you. But I think you should know. Gabriela said that she had to leave."

"Why?" Riley gasped.

Ryan looked confused. "Aren't you paying her enough?" he asked.

"It was because of me," April said. "She said she couldn't do it anymore. She said it was too much responsibility for her to have to stop me from harming myself or getting myself killed."

April paused. A tear came to her eye.

"She said it was too easy for me to sneak out without her knowing. She couldn't sleep at night wondering if I was putting myself in danger. She said that now that I was healthy again, she was moving out right away."

Riley was jolted with alarm. She'd had no idea that Gabriela had been thinking any such thing.

"I begged her not to go," April said. "I was crying and she was crying, too. But I couldn't change her mind, and I was terrified."

April choked back a sob and wiped her eyes with a tissue.

"Mom," April said, "I actually got down on my knees. I promised never, ever to make her feel that way again. Finally … *finally* she hugged me and said she wouldn't leave as long as I kept my promise. And I will. I really will. Mom, Dad, I'll never make you or Gabriela or anybody worry about me like that ever again."

Dr. Sloat patted April's hand and smiled at Riley and Ryan.

She said, "I guess what April's trying to say is that she's turned a corner."

Riley saw Ryan take out a handkerchief and dab his eyes. She'd very rarely ever seen him cry. But she understood how he felt. She felt her own throat catch. It was Gabriela—not Riley or Ryan—who had made April see the light.

Even so, Riley felt incredibly grateful that her family would be together and in good health for Christmas. She ignored the dread that lurked deep down inside, the awful feeling that the monsters in her life were going to take away her holiday.

CHAPTER THREE

When Shane Hatcher walked into the prison library on Christmas Day, the wall clock showed that it was exactly two minutes before the hour.

Perfect timing, he thought.

In a few minutes, he was going to break free.

He was amused to see Christmas decorations hung here and there—all made of colored Styrofoam, of course, nothing hard or with edges or useful as rope. Hatcher had spent a lot of Christmas holidays in Sing Sing, and the idea of trying to evoke the holiday spirit here always struck him as absurd. He almost laughed aloud when he saw Freddy, the taciturn prison librarian, wearing a red Santa hat.

Sitting at his desk, Freddy turned toward him and smiled a cadaverous smile. That smile told Hatcher that everything was set to go as planned. Hatcher silently nodded and smiled back at him. Then Hatcher walked between two shelves and waited.

Just as the clock ticked the hour, Hatcher heard the sound of the loading dock door opening at the far end of the library. In just a few moments, a truck driver came in pushing a large plastic bin on wheels. The dock door closed noisily behind him.

"Whatcha got for me this week, Bader?" Freddy asked.

"What do you think I've got?" the driver said. "Books, books, books."

The driver took a quick peek in Hatcher's direction, then turned away. The driver, of course, was in on the plan. From that moment on, both the driver and Freddy treated Hatcher as if he weren't there at all.

Excellent, Hatcher thought.

Together, Bader and Freddy unloaded the books onto a wheeled steel table.

"How's about a cup of coffee over in the commissary?" Freddy said to the driver. "Or maybe some hot eggnog? They're serving it for the holiday."

"Sounds great."

The two men chatted casually as they disappeared through the swinging double doors out of the library.

Hatcher stood quietly for a moment, studying the exact position of the bin. He'd paid off a guard to nudge a surveillance camera little by little over a period of days until there was a blind spot in the library—one that the guards who watched the monitors hadn't yet noticed. It looked like the driver had hit the mark perfectly.

Hatcher silently stepped out from between the shelves and climbed inside the bin. The driver had left a coarse, heavy packing blanket at the bottom. Hatcher pulled the blanket over himself.

Now was the only phase of Hatcher's plan when he thought that anything could possibly go wrong. But even if somebody came into the library, he doubted that they would bother to look inside the bin. Others who might ordinarily have checked the book truck closely as it left had been paid off too.

Not that he was worried or nervous. He hadn't felt such emotions for some three decades now. A man who had nothing to lose in life had no cause for anxiety or unease. The only thing that could arouse his interest was the promise of the unknown.

He lay underneath the blanket, listening closely. He heard the wall clock tick the minute.

Five more minutes, he thought.

That was the plan. Those five minutes would give Freddy deniability. He could honestly say that he hadn't seen Hatcher climb into the bin. He could say he'd thought Hatcher had actually left the library earlier. When five minutes were up, Freddy and the driver would return, and Hatcher would be carted out of the library and then driven out of the prison.

Meanwhile, Hatcher allowed his thoughts to stray to what he was going to do with his freedom. He had recently heard some news that made the risk worthwhile—even interesting.

Hatcher smiled when he thought about another person who would take keen interest in his escape. He wished he could see Riley Paige's face when she found out he was at large.

He chuckled ever so softly.

It was going to be nice to see her again.

CHAPTER FOUR

Riley watched as April opened the box containing the Christmas present that Ryan had bought for her. She wondered just how in tune Ryan was with his daughter's taste these days.

April smiled as she took out a bangle bracelet.

"It's beautiful, Daddy!" she said, giving him a kiss on the cheek.

"I hear it's quite the style these days," Ryan said.

"It is!" April said. "Thanks!"

Then she gave Riley a barely noticeable wink. Riley suppressed a chuckle. Just a few days ago, April had told Riley how much she hated these silly bracelets that all the girls were wearing. In spite of that, April was doing a great job of acting enthusiastic.

Of course, Riley knew that it wasn't entirely an act. She could see that April was pleased that her father had at least made an effort to buy a Christmas present that she would like.

Riley felt much the same way about the expensive handbag Ryan had bought for her. It wasn't her style at all, and she'd never use it—except when she knew Ryan would be around. And for all she knew, Ryan felt exactly the same way about the wallet she and April had bought for him.

We're trying to be a family again, Riley thought.

And for the moment, they seemed to be succeeding.

It was Christmas morning, and Ryan had just come over to spend the day with them. Riley, April, Ryan, and Gabriela were all sitting near the roaring fireplace sipping on hot chocolate. The delicious smell of Gabriela's grand Christmas dinner wafted in from the kitchen.

Riley, April, and Ryan were all wearing the scarves that Gabriela had made for them, and Gabriela was wearing fluffy slippers that April and Riley had bought for her.

The doorbell rang, and Riley went over to answer it. Her neighbor, Blaine, and his teenage daughter, Crystal, were standing outside.

Riley was at once delighted and uneasy to see them. In the past, Ryan had shown more than a little jealousy toward Blaine—and not without reason, Riley had to admit. The truth was, she found him quite attractive.

Riley couldn't help mentally comparing him to both Bill and Ryan. Blaine was a couple of years younger than she was, lean and fit, and she liked the fact that he wasn't vain enough to disguise his receding hairline.

"Come on in!" Riley said.

"Sorry, I can't," Blaine said. "I've got to get over to the restaurant. I brought Crystal by, though."

Blaine owned a popular restaurant downtown. Riley realized that she shouldn't be surprised that it was open on Christmas day. Today's holiday dinner at Blaine's Grill must be delicious.

Crystal hurried inside and joined the group at the fireplace. Giggling, she and April immediately tore into presents they had bought for each other.

Riley and Blaine discreetly exchanged their Christmas cards, then Blaine left. When Riley rejoined the group, Ryan was looking rather sour. Riley tucked the card away without opening it. She'd wait until after Ryan was gone.

My life certainly is complicated, she thought. But it was beginning to feel like an almost normal life, a version of life that she could enjoy.

*

Riley's footsteps echoed through a large dark room. Suddenly, there came the noisy crack of breaker switches. Lights came on, blinding her for a few seconds.

Riley found herself in the corridor of what seemed to be a wax museum filled with grisly exhibits. To her right was a naked woman's corpse, splayed doll-like against a tree. To her left was a dead woman wrapped in chains and hanging from a lamppost. An exhibit farther on displayed several women's corpses with their arms bound behind their backs. Beyond that were starved dead bodies with their limbs grotesquely arranged.

Riley recognized every scene. They were all cases she had worked on in the past. She had entered her own personal chamber of horrors.

But what was she doing here?

Suddenly she heard a young voice call out with terror.

"Riley, help me!"

She looked straight ahead and saw the silhouette of a young girl holding out her arms in desperate appeal.

It looked like Jilly. She was in trouble again.

Riley broke into a run toward her. But then another light came on and showed that the silhouette wasn't Jilly at all.

It was a grizzled old man wearing the full dress uniform of a Marine colonel.

It was Riley's own father. And he was laughing at Riley's mistake.

"You didn't expect to find anybody alive, did you?" he said. "You're no good to anybody unless they're dead. How many times do I have to tell you?"

Riley was puzzled. Her father had died months ago. She didn't miss him. She did her best never to think about him. He'd always been a hard man who had never given her anything but pain.

"What are you doing here?" Riley asked.

"Just passing through." He chuckled. "Checking in to see how you're botching your life. Same as always, I see."

Riley wanted to lunge at him. She wanted hit him as hard as she could. But she found herself frozen where she stood.

Then came a loud buzzing sound.

"Wish we could chat," he said. "But you've got other business."

The buzzing became louder and louder. Her father turned and walked away.

"You never did anybody a lick of good," he said. "Not even yourself."

Riley's eyes snapped open. She realized that her phone was ringing. The clock showed that it was 6:00 a.m.

She saw that the call was from Quantico. A call at this hour had to mean something dire.

She answered the phone and heard the stern voice of her team chief, Special Agent in Charge Brent Meredith.

"Agent Paige, I need you in my office right now," he said. "That's an order."

Riley rubbed her eyes.

"What's it about?" she asked.

There was a short pause.

"We'll have to discuss it in person," he said.

He ended the call. For a groggy moment, Riley wondered if she might be in for a reprimand for her behavior. But no, she'd been off duty for months now. A call from Meredith could only mean one thing.

It's a case, Riley thought.

He wouldn't call her on a holiday for any other reason.

And from Meredith's tone of voice, she felt sure it was going to be big—maybe even life-changing.

CHAPTER FIVE

Riley's apprehension mounted as she entered the BAU building. When she walked into Brent Meredith's office, the chief was at his desk waiting for her. A big man with angular, African-American features, Meredith was always an imposing presence. Right now he also looked worried.

Bill was there as well. Riley could see by his expression that he didn't yet know what the meeting was about.

"Have a seat, Agent Paige," Meredith said.

Riley sat down in a free chair.

"I'm sorry to interrupt your holidays," Meredith said to Riley. "It's been a while since we've talked. How are you doing?"

Riley was taken aback. It wasn't Meredith's style to start a meeting this way—with an apology and a query about her well-being. He normally got right to the point. Of course, he knew that she'd been on leave because of the crisis with April. Riley understood that Meredith was genuinely concerned. Even so, this struck her as odd.

"I'm doing better, thanks," she said.

"And your daughter?" Meredith asked.

"She's recovering well, thank you," Riley said.

Meredith fixed his gaze on her in silence for a moment.

"I hope you're ready to come back to work," Meredith said. "Because if we've ever needed you on a case, it's this one."

Riley's imagination boggled as she waited for him to explain.

Finally, Meredith said, "Shane Hatcher has escaped from the Sing Sing Correctional Facility."

His words hit her like a ton of bricks. Riley was glad she was sitting down.

"My God," Bill said, looking equally stunned.

Riley knew Shane Hatcher well—too well for her own liking. He had been serving life without possibility of parole for decades now. During his time in prison, he'd become an expert in criminology. He'd published articles in scholarly magazines and had actually taught classes in the prison's academic programs. Several times now, Riley had visited him in Sing Sing, seeking advice on current cases.

The visits had always been disturbing. Hatcher seemed to feel a special affinity for her. And Riley knew that, deep down, she was more fascinated with him than she ought to be. She thought that he was probably the most intelligent man that she had ever met—and also probably the most dangerous.

She'd sworn after every visit never to see him again. Now she remembered all too well the last time she'd left the Sing Sing visiting room.

"I won't come back here to see you again," she'd told him.

"You might not have to come back here to see me," he'd replied.

Now those words seemed disturbingly prescient.

"How did he escape?" Riley asked Meredith.

"I don't have many details," Meredith said. "But as you probably know, he spent a lot of time in the prison library, and he often worked there as an assistant. Yesterday he was there when a book delivery came in. He must have slipped away on the truck that brought the books. Late last night, about the time guards noticed that he was missing, the truck was found abandoned a few miles outside of Ossining. There was no sign of the driver."

Meredith fell silent again. Riley could easily believe that Hatcher had staged such a daring escape. As for the driver, Riley hated to think of what might have become of him.

Meredith leaned across his desk toward Riley.

"Agent Paige, you know Hatcher better than maybe anybody else. What can you tell us about him?"

Still reeling from the news, Riley took a deep breath.

She said, "In his youth, Hatcher was a gangbanger in Syracuse. He was unusually vicious even for a hardened criminal. People called him 'Shane the Chain' because he liked to beat gang rivals to death with chains."

Riley paused, remembering what Shane had told her.

"A certain beat cop made it his personal mission to bring Hatcher down. Hatcher retaliated by pulverizing him to an unrecognizable pulp with tire chains. He left his mangled body on his front porch for his family to find. That's when Hatcher got caught. He's been in prison now for thirty years. He was never supposed to get out."

Another silence fell.

"He's fifty-five years old now," Meredith said. "I'd think that after thirty years in prison, he wouldn't be as dangerous as he was when he was young."

Riley shook her head.

"You'd be thinking wrong," she said. "Back then, he was just an ignorant punk. He had no idea of his own potential. But over the years he's acquired a vast store of knowledge. He knows he's a genius. And he's never shown any real remorse. Oh, he's developed a polished persona over the years. And he's behaved himself in prison—it gets him privileges even if it won't shorten his sentence. But I'm sure he's more vicious and dangerous than ever."

Riley thought for a moment. Something was bothering her. She couldn't quite put her finger on it.

"Does anybody know why?" she asked.

"Why what?" Bill said.

"Why he escaped."

Bill and Meredith exchanged puzzled looks.

"Why does anybody escape from prison?" Bill asked.

Riley understood how strange her question sounded. She remembered one time when Bill went with her to talk with Hatcher.

"Bill, you met him," she said. "Did he strike you as—well, dissatisfied? Restless?"

Bill knitted his brow in thought.

"No, actually he seemed …"

His voice trailed off.

"Almost contented, maybe?" Riley said, finishing his thought. "Prison seems to suit him. I've never gotten the feeling that he even wants freedom. There's something almost Zen-like about him, his non-attachment to anything in life. He's got no desires that I know of. Freedom has nothing to offer him that he wants. And now he's on the run, a wanted man. So why did he decide to escape? And why now?"

Meredith drummed his fingers on his desk.

"How did you leave things the last time you saw him?" he asked. "Did you part on good terms?"

Riley barely suppressed a wry smile.

"We never part on good terms," she said.

Then after a pause, she added, "I understand what you're getting at. You're wondering if I'm his target."

"Is it possible?" Bill asked.

Riley didn't reply. Again, she remembered what Hatcher had said to her.

"You might not have to come back here to see me."

Had it been a threat? Riley didn't know.

Meredith said, "Agent Paige, I don't need to tell you that this is going to be a high-pressure, high-profile case. Even as we speak, news is getting out to the media. Prison escapes are always big news. They can even cause public panic. Whatever it is he's up to, we've got to stop him fast. I wish you didn't have to come back to a

24

case this dangerous and hard. Do you feel ready? Do you feel up to it?"

Riley felt a strange tingling as she thought about the question. It was a feeling that she'd seldom if ever felt before taking on a case. It took her a moment to realize that the feeling was fear, pure and simple.

But it wasn't fear for her own safety. It was something else. It was something unnamable and irrational. Perhaps it was the fact that Hatcher knew her so well. In her experience, all prisoners wanted something in return for information. But Hatcher hadn't been interested in the usual little offerings of whiskey or cigarettes. His own *quid pro quo* had been both simple and deeply unsettling.

He'd wanted her to tell him things about her.

"Something that you don't want people to know," he'd said. *"Something you wouldn't want anybody to know."*

Riley had complied, maybe too readily. Now Hatcher knew all sorts of things about her—that she was a flawed mother, that she hated her father and didn't go to his funeral, that there was sexual tension between her and Bill, and that sometimes—like Hatcher himself—she took great pleasure in violence and killing.

She remembered what he'd said during their last visit.

"I know you. In some ways, I know you better than you know yourself."

Could she really match wits with such a man? Meredith was sitting there, patiently awaiting an answer to his question.

"I'm as ready as I can be," she said, trying to sound more confident than she felt.

"Good," Meredith said. "How do you think we should proceed?"

Riley thought for a moment.

"Bill and I need to look at all the information on Shane Hatcher that the Agency has on hand," she said.

Meredith nodded and said, "I've already got Sam Flores setting things up."

*

A few minutes later, Riley, Bill, and Meredith were in the BAU conference room looking at the huge multimedia display that Sam Flores had put together. Flores was a lab technician with black-rimmed glasses.

25

"I think I've got everything you could possibly want to see," Flores said. "Birth certificate, arrest records, court transcripts, the works."

Riley saw that it was an impressive display. And it certainly didn't leave much to the imagination. There were several gruesome photos of Shane Hatcher's murdered victims, including the mangled cop lying on his own front porch.

"What information do we have about the cop Hatcher killed?" Bill asked.

Flores brought up a batch of photos of a hearty-looking police officer.

"We're talking about Officer Lucien Wayles, forty-six years old when he died in 1986," Flores said. "He was married with three kids, awarded a Medal of Valor, well-liked and respected. The FBI teamed up with local cops and nailed Hatcher within days after Wayles was killed. What's amazing is that they didn't beat Hatcher to a pulp right then and there."

Scanning the display, Riley was most struck by the photos of Hatcher himself. She barely recognized him. Although the man she knew could be intimidating, he managed to project a respectable, even bookish demeanor, with a pair of reading glasses always perched on his nose. The young African American in the 1986 mugshots had a lean, hard face and a cruel, empty stare. Riley had a hard time believing that it was the same person.

As detailed and complete as the display was, Riley felt dissatisfied. She had thought that she knew Shane Hatcher as well as anybody alive. But she didn't know *this* Shane Hatcher—the vicious young gangbanger called "Shane the Chain."

I've got to get to know him, she thought.

Otherwise, she doubted that she could possibly catch him.

Somehow, she felt that the cold, digital feeling of the display was working against her. She needed something more tangible—actual glossy photographs with folds and frayed edges, yellowed and brittle reports and documents.

She asked Flores, "Could I get a look at the originals of these materials?"

Flores let out a slight snort of disbelief.

"Sorry, Agent Paige—but not a chance. The FBI shredded all its paper files in 2014. Now all of it is scanned and digitized. What you see is all we've got."

Riley let out a sigh of disappointment. Yes, she remembered all that shredding of millions of paper files. Other agents had complained, but back then it hadn't seemed like a problem to her. Now she fairly itched for some old-fashioned palpability.

But right now, the important thing was to figure out Hatcher's next move. An idea occurred to her.

"Who was the cop who brought Hatcher in?" she asked. "If he's still alive, Hatcher's liable to target him first."

"It wasn't a local cop," Flores said. "And it wasn't a 'he.'"

He brought up an old photo of a woman agent.

"Her name was Kelsey Sprigge. She was an FBI agent at the Syracuse office—was thirty-five years old at the time. She's seventy now, retired and living in Searcy, a town near Syracuse."

Riley was surprised that Sprigge was a woman.

"She must have joined the bureau—" Riley began.

Flores continued her thought.

"She signed up in 1972, when J. Edgar's corpse was barely cold. That was when women were finally allowed to apply to be agents. She'd been a local cop before then."

Riley was impressed. Kelsey Sprigge had lived a lot of history.

"What can you tell me about her?" Riley asked Flores.

"Well, she's a widow with three children and three grandchildren."

"Call the Syracuse FBI field office and tell them to do whatever they can to keep Sprigge safe," Riley said. "She's in serious danger."

Flores nodded.

Then she turned to Meredith.

"Sir, I'm going to need a plane."

"Why?" he asked, confused.

She took a deep breath.

"Shane may be on his way to kill Sprigge," she said. "And I want to see her first."

CHAPTER SIX

As the FBI jet hit the runway at Syracuse Hancock International Airport, Riley remembered something her father had told her in last night's dream.

"You're no good to anybody unless they're dead."

Riley was struck by the irony. This was perhaps the first case she'd ever been assigned where somebody hadn't been murdered already.

But that's likely to change soon, she thought.

She was especially worried about Kelsey Sprigge. She wanted to meet the woman face to face and see that she was all right. Then it would be up to Riley and Bill to keep her that way, and that would mean tracking down Shane Hatcher and putting him back in prison.

As the plane taxied toward the terminal, Riley saw that they had traveled into a true winter world. Although the landing strip was clear, huge mountains of snow showed how much work the plows had put in recently.

It was a change of scenery from Virginia—and a welcome one. Now Riley realized how much she needed a new challenge. She had called Gabriela from Quantico to explain that she was on her way to work on a case. Gabriela had been happy for her and assured her that she'd take care of April.

When the plane came to a stop, Riley and Bill grabbed their gear and climbed down the stairs onto the icy tarmac. When she felt the shock of deep cold on her face, she was glad that she'd been issued a heavy hooded jacket at Quantico.

Two men scurried toward them and introduced themselves as Agents McGill and Newton of the FBI field office in Syracuse.

"We're here to help any way we can," McGill told Bill and Riley as they all hurried into the terminal.

Riley asked the first question that came to her mind.

"Have you got people watching Kelsey Sprigge? Are you sure she's safe?"

"Some local cops are posted outside her house in Searcy," Newton said. "We're sure she's fine."

Riley wished she felt as certain.

Bill said, "Okay then. Right now we just need something to drive to Searcy."

McGill said, "Searcy's not far from Syracuse, and the roads are all clear. We've brought an SUV you can use, but … uh, are you used to driving in northern winters?"

"You know, Syracuse always wins the Golden Snowball Award," Newton added with impish pride.

"Golden Snowball?" Riley asked.

"That's New York state's prize for the most snow," McGill said. "We're the champs. Got a trophy to prove it."

"Maybe one of us should drive you," Newton said.

Bill chuckled. "Thanks, but I think we can handle it. I had a winter assignment in North Dakota a few years ago. I got a good dose of winter driving there."

Although she didn't say so, Riley also felt seasoned for this kind of driving. She'd learned to drive in the Virginia mountains. The snow there was never as deep as it was here, but the back roads were never cleared very quickly. She'd probably put in as much time on icy roads as anybody here.

But she was happy to have Bill drive. Right now she was preoccupied with Kelsey Sprigge's safety. Bill took the keys and they were on their way.

"I've got to say, it feels good to be working together again," Bill said as he drove. "It's selfish of me, I guess. I like working with Lucy, but it's not the same."

Riley smiled. She also felt good to be working with Bill again.

"Still, part of me wishes you weren't coming back to this case," Bill added.

"Why not?" Riley asked with surprise.

Bill shook his head.

"I've just got a bad feeling," he said. "Remember, I met Hatcher too. It takes a lot to scare me, but … well, he's in a class by himself."

Riley didn't reply, but she couldn't disagree. She knew that Hatcher had pushed Bill's buttons during that visit. With uncanny instinct, the longtime prisoner had made shrewd observations about Bill's personal life.

Riley remembered how Hatcher had pointed to Bill's wedding band and said:

"Forget about trying to fix things with your wife. It can't be done."

Hatcher had been right, and Bill was now in the middle of an ugly divorce.

At the end of the same visit, he'd said something to Riley that still haunted her.

"Stop fighting it."

To this day, she didn't know what Hatcher had meant she should stop fighting. But she felt an inexplicable dread that one day she was going to find out.

*

A little while later, Bill parked alongside a huge pile of plowed snow outside Kelsey Sprigge's house in Searcy. Riley saw a police car parked nearby with a couple of uniformed cops inside. But two cops in a car didn't inspire her with a whole lot of confidence. The vicious and brilliant criminal who had broken out of Sing Sing could make short work of them if he put his mind to it.

Bill and Riley got out of the car and flashed their badges at the cops. Then they walked up the shoveled sidewalk toward the house. It was a traditional two-story home with a practical pitched roof and enclosed front porch, and it was covered with Christmas lights. Riley rang the doorbell.

A woman answered the door with a charming smile. She was lean and fit and wearing a jogging suit. Her expression was bright and cheerful.

"Why, you must be Agents Jeffreys and Paige," she said. "I'm Kelsey Sprigge. Come on in. Get out of this awful cold."

Kelsey Sprigge led Riley and Bill to a cozy living room with a roaring fire.

"Would you like something to drink?" she asked. "Of course, you're on duty. I'll get some coffee."

She went into the kitchen, and Bill and Riley sat down. Riley looked around at the Christmas decorations and at the dozens of framed photographs hanging from the walls and resting on the furniture. They were taken of Kelsey Sprigge at various times of her adult life, with children and grandchildren all around her. In many of the pictures, a smiling man stood at her side.

Riley remembered that Flores had said she was a widow. From the photos Riley guessed that it had been a long, happy marriage. Somehow, Kelsey Sprigge had managed to accomplish something that had always defeated Riley. She had lived a full, loving family life while working as an FBI agent.

Riley more than half wanted to ask her how she'd managed that. But of course, now was not the time.

The woman quickly returned carrying a tray with two cups of coffee, cream and sugar, and—to Riley's surprise—a scotch on the rocks for herself.

Riley was in awe of Kelsey. For a woman of seventy, she was extremely spry and full of life, and tougher than most women she'd met. In some ways, Riley felt it was like looking at a sneak preview of the woman she might become.

"Well, now," Kelsey said, sitting down and smiling. "I wish our weather was more welcoming."

Riley was startled by her easy hospitality. Under the circumstances, she thought that the woman should be truly alarmed.

"Ms. Sprigge—" Bill began.

"Kelsey, please," the woman interrupted. "And I know why you're here. You're worried that Shane Hatcher might be coming after me, that I might be his first target. You think he wants to murder me."

Riley and Bill looked at each other, not sure what to say.

"And of course, that's why those police are outside," Kelsey said, still smiling sweetly. "I asked them to come in and warm up, but they wouldn't do it. They wouldn't even let me go out for my afternoon jog! Such a shame, I just love getting out for a run in this brisk weather. Well, I'm not worried about being murdered, and I don't think you should worry either. I really don't think that Shane Hatcher intends to do any such thing."

Riley almost blurted, *"Why not?"*

Instead, she said cautiously, "Kelsey, you captured him. You brought him to justice. He was spending his life in prison because of you. You might be the whole reason he got out."

Kelsey didn't say anything for a moment. She was eyeing the pistol in Riley's holster.

"What weapon do you carry, dear?" she asked.

"A forty-caliber Glock," Riley said.

"Nice!" Kelsey said. "May I have a look at it?"

Riley handed Kelsey her weapon. Kelsey took out the magazine and examined the gun. She handled it with the appreciation of a connoisseur.

"Glocks came along a little too late for me to use in the field," she said. "I like them, though. The polymer frame has a good feel to it—very light, excellent balance. I love the sighting arrangement."

She put the magazine back in and handed the gun back to Riley. Then she walked over to a desk. She took out a semiautomatic pistol of her own.

"I took Shane Hatcher down with this baby," she said, smiling. She handed the gun to Riley, then sat back down. "Smith and Wesson Model 459. I wounded and disarmed him. My partner wanted to kill him on the spot—revenge for the cop he'd killed.

31

Well, I wouldn't have it. I told him if he did kill Hatcher, there'd be more than one corpse to bury."

Kelsey blushed a little.

"Oh, dear," she said. "I'd rather that story didn't get around. Please don't tell anybody."

Riley handed the weapon back to her.

"Anyway, I could tell that I met with Hatcher's approval," Kelsey said. "You know, he had a strict code, even as a gangbanger. He knew that I was just doing my job. I think he respected that. And he was grateful, too. Anyway, he's never shown any interest in me. I even wrote him a few letters, but he never wrote back. He probably doesn't even remember my name. No, I'm all but positive he doesn't want to kill me."

Kelsey peered at Riley with interest.

"But Riley—is it OK for me to call you Riley?—you told me on the phone that you'd actually visited him, that you'd gotten to know him. He must be quite fascinating."

Riley thought she actually detected a note of envy in the woman's voice.

Kelsey rose from her chair.

"But listen to me babble, while you've got a bad guy to catch! And who knows what he might be up to, even as we speak. I've got some information that might help. Come on, I'll show you everything I've got."

She led Riley and Bill through a hallway to a basement door. Riley's nerves quickened.

Why does it have to be in a basement? she thought.

Riley had harbored a slight but irrational phobia about basements for some time now—vestiges of PTSD from having been held captive in Peterson's damp crawlspace, and even more recently from having taken out a different killer in a pitch-dark basement.

But as they followed Kelsey down the stairs, Riley saw nothing sinister. The basement was finished as a comfortable rec room. In one corner was a well-lighted office area with a desk covered with manila folders, a bulletin board with old photographs and newspaper clippings, and a couple of filing drawers.

"Here it is—everything you could want to know about 'Shane the Chain' and his career and downfall," Kelsey said. "Help yourself. Ask if you need help making sense out of it all."

Riley and Bill started looking through folders. Riley was surprised and thrilled. It was a fascinating, even daunting body of information and a lot of it had never been scanned for the FBI database. The folder she was looking through was crammed with seemingly unimportant items, including restaurant napkins with handwritten notes and sketches pertaining to the case.

She opened another folder that held photocopied reports and other documents. Riley was a bit amused to realize that Kelsey surely wasn't supposed to have copied or kept them. The originals had surely long since been shredded after being scanned.

As Bill and Riley pored over the material, Kelsey remarked, "I guess you're wondering why I just won't let this case go. Sometimes I wonder myself."

She thought for a moment.

"Shane Hatcher was my one brush with real evil," she said. "During my first fourteen years with the Bureau, I was pretty much window dressing here in the Syracuse office—the token woman. But I worked this case from the ground up, talking to gangbangers in the street, taking charge of the team. Nobody thought I could bring Hatcher down. In fact, nobody was sure that anybody could bring him down. But I did."

Now Riley was looking through a folder of poor-quality photos that the Bureau probably hadn't bothered to scan. Kelsey had obviously known better than to throw them away.

One showed a cop sitting in a café talking to a gangbanger. Riley immediately recognized the young man as Shane Hatcher. It took her a moment to recognize the cop.

"That's the officer that Hatcher killed, isn't it?" Riley said.

Kelsey nodded.

"Officer Lucien Wayles," she said. "I took that photograph myself."

"What's he doing talking with Hatcher?"

Kelsey smiled knowingly.

"Well, now, that's rather interesting," she said. "I suppose you've heard that Officer Wayles was an upstanding, decorated policeman. That's what the local cops still want everybody to think. Actually, he was corrupt to the very bone. In this picture, he was meeting with Hatcher hoping to make a deal with him—a cut of the drug profits for not interfering with Hatcher's territory. Hatcher said no. That's when Wayles decided to do Hatcher in."

Kelsey pulled out a photograph of Wayles's mangled body.

"As you probably know, that didn't work out too well for Officer Wayles," she said.

Riley felt a tingle of understanding. This was exactly the treasure trove of material she'd yearned for. It brought her much, much closer to the mind of the youthful Shane Hatcher.

As she looked at the photo of Hatcher and the cop, Riley probed the young man's mind. She imagined Hatcher's thoughts and feelings at the moment the picture was taken. She also remembered something that Kelsey had just said.

"You know, he had a strict code, even as a gangbanger."

From her own conversations with Hatcher, Riley knew that it was still true today. And now, looking at the photo, Riley could feel Hatcher's visceral disgust at Wayles's proposal.

It offended him, Riley thought. *It felt like an insult.*

Small wonder that Hatcher had made such a gruesome example of Wayles. According to Hatcher's twisted code, it was the moral thing to do.

Thumbing through more photos, Riley found a mugshot of another gangbanger.

"Who's this?" Riley asked.

"Smokey Moran," Kelsey said. "Shane the Chain's most trusted lieutenant—until I busted him for selling drugs. He faced a long prison sentence, so I had no trouble getting him to turn state's evidence against Hatcher in return for some leniency. That's how I finally nailed Hatcher."

Riley's skin prickled as she handled the picture.

"What became of Moran?" she asked.

Kelsey shook her head with disapproval.

"He's still out there," she said. "I often wish I hadn't made that deal. For years and years now, he's been quietly running all kinds of gang activities. The younger gangbangers look up to him and admire him. He's smart and elusive. The local cops and the Bureau have never been able to bring him to justice."

That prickling feeling grew. Riley found herself in Hatcher's mind, brooding in prison for decades over Moran's betrayal. In Hatcher's moral universe, such a man didn't deserve to live. And justice was long overdue.

"Do you have his current address?" Riley asked Kelsey.

"No, but I'm sure the field office does. Why?"

Riley took a deep breath.

"Because Shane is going there to kill him."

CHAPTER SEVEN

Riley knew that Smokey Moran was in great danger. But the truth was, Riley's heart didn't exactly go out to the vicious career thug.

Shane Hatcher was what really mattered.

Her assignment was to put Hatcher back in prison. If they caught him before he killed Moran for the old betrayal, fine. She and Bill would drive to Moran's address without giving him any advance warning. They would call the local field office to have backup meet them there.

It was about a half hour drive from Kelsey Sprigge's home in middle-class Searcy to the much more sinister gang neighborhoods of Syracuse. The sky was overcast, but no snow was falling, and traffic moved normally along the well-cleared roads.

As Bill drove, Riley accessed the FBI database and did some quick research on her cell phone. She saw that the local gang situation was dire. Gangs had grouped and regrouped in this area since the early 1980s. Back in the era of Shane the Chain, they had been mostly locals. Since then national gangs had moved in, bringing with them heightened levels of violence.

The drugs that fueled this violence with their profits had gotten weirder and much more dangerous. They now included cigarettes soaked in embalming fluid and paranoia-inducing crystals called "bath salts." Who knew what even deadlier substances would turn up next?

As Bill parked in front of the rundown apartment building where Moran lived, Riley saw two men wearing FBI jackets get out of another car—Agents McGill and Newton, who had met them at the airport. She could tell from their bulkiness that they were wearing Kevlar vests under the jackets. Both were carrying Remington sniper rifles.

"Moran's place is on the third floor," Riley said.

When the group of agents moved in through the building's front door, they encountered several gangbanger types standing around in the cold and shabby foyer. They just stood there with their hands shoved into their hoodie pockets and appeared to pay little attention to the armed squad.

Moran's bodyguards?

She didn't think they were likely to try to stop her little army of agents, although they might signal Moran that someone was on the way up.

McGill and Newton appeared to know the young guys. The agents patted them down quickly.

"We're here to see Smokey Moran," Riley said.

None of the young men said a word. They just stared at the agents with strange, empty expressions. It struck Riley as odd behavior.

"Out," said Newton, and the guys nodded in compliance and filed out the front door.

With Riley in the lead, the agents stormed up three flights of stairs. The local agents led the way, checking each hallway carefully. On the third floor, they stopped outside Moran's apartment.

Riley knocked sharply on the door. When no one answered, she called out.

"Smokey Moran, this is FBI Agent Riley Paige. My colleagues and I need to have a word with you. We don't mean you any harm. We're not here to arrest you."

Again came no answer.

"We have reason to believe that your life is in danger," Riley shouted.

Still no answer.

Riley turned the doorknob. To her surprise, it wasn't locked, and the door swung open.

The agents stepped into a neatly kept, nondescript apartment with virtually no decor. There was also no TV, no electronic devices, certainly no sign of a computer. Riley realized that Moran managed to wield tremendous influence in the criminal underworld solely by giving face-to-face orders. By never going online or even using a phone, he stayed under law enforcement's radar.

Definitely a shrewd customer, Riley thought. *Sometimes the old-fashioned way works best.*

But he was nowhere in sight. The two local agents quickly checked all the rooms and closets. Nobody was in the apartment.

They all made their way back down the stairs. When they reached the foyer, McGill and Newton lifted their rifles, ready for action. The young gangbangers awaited them at the base of the stairs.

Riley looked them over. She realized they'd obviously been under orders to let Riley and her colleagues search the empty apartment. Now it seemed that they had something to say.

"Smokey said he thought you'd come," one of the gangbangers said.

"He told us to give you a message," another said.

"He said to look for him over at the old Bushnell Warehouse on Dolliver Street," a third said.

Then, without another word, the young men stepped aside, leaving the agents plenty of room to leave.

"Was he alone?" Riley asked.

"Was when he left here," one of the young men replied.

A sort of solemn foreboding hung in the air. Riley didn't know what to make of it.

McGill and Newton kept their eyes on the young guys as the agents exited. When they got outside, Newton said, "I know where that warehouse is."

"I do too," McGill said. "It's just a few blocks from here. It's abandoned and up for sale, and there's been talk of turning it into classy apartments. But I don't like the sound of this. That place is perfect for an ambush."

He got on his phone and requested more backup to meet them there.

"We'll have to be careful," Riley said. "Lead the way."

Bill drove, following the local SUV. Both cars parked in front of a decrepit four-story brick building with a crumbling facade and broken windows. As they did, another FBI vehicle pulled up.

Looking over the building, Riley could see what McGill had meant and why he had wanted more backup. The place was huge and decrepit with three floors of dark and broken windows. Any of those windows could easily hide a shooter with a rifle.

All of the local team was armed with long guns, but she and Bill had only pistols. They might be sitting ducks in a firefight.

Still, an ambush didn't make sense to her. After shrewdly evading arrest for some three decades, why would a guy as bright as Smokey Moran do something reckless like gun down FBI agents?

Riley called the other agents on her radio.

"You guys still wearing Kevlar?" she asked.

"Yeah," came the reply.

"Good. Stay put in your car until I tell you to come out."

Bill had already reached into the back of their well-stocked SUV, where he had found two Kevlar vests. He and Riley quickly slipped into them. Then Riley found a megaphone.

She rolled down the window and called out to the building.

"Smokey Moran, we're FBI. We got your message. We came to see you. We don't mean you any harm. Come out of the building with your hands up and let's talk."

She waited for a full minute. Nothing happened.

Riley got on the radio again to Newton and McGill.

"Agent Jeffreys and I are getting out of our vehicle. When we're out, you get out too—with your weapons drawn. We'll all meet at the front door. Keep your eyes high. If you see any movement anywhere in the building, take immediate cover."

Riley and Bill got out of the SUV, and Newton and McGill got out of their car. Three more heavily armed FBI agents got out of the newly arrived vehicle and joined them.

The agents moved cautiously toward the building, eyeing the windows with their guns ready. Finally they reached the relative safety of the enormous front doorway.

"What's the plan?" McGill asked, sounding distinctly nervous.

"To arrest Shane Harris, if he's in there," Riley said. "To kill him if necessary. And to find Smokey Moran."

Bill added, "We'll have to search the whole building."

Riley could tell that the local agents didn't much like this plan. She couldn't blame them.

"McGill," she said, "start on the ground floor, working your way up. Jeffreys and I will head to the top floor and work our way down. We'll meet in the middle."

McGill nodded. Riley could see a flash of relief on his face. They clearly knew that danger was much less likely in the lower part of the building. Bill and Riley would be putting themselves at considerably greater risk.

Newton said, "I'm going up with you."

She saw that his expression was firm and made no objection.

Bill pushed the doors open, and all five agents went inside. Icy wind whistled through the windows of the bottom floor, which was mostly an empty space with posts and doors to several adjoining rooms. Leaving McGill and three others to start down here, Riley and Bill headed for the more threatening stairwell. Newton followed closely behind them.

Despite the cold, she could feel sweat in her gloves and on her forehead. She felt her heart pounding and worked hard to keep her breathing under control. No matter how many times she'd do this, she'd never get used to it. Nobody could.

At last they entered the vast, loft-like upper story.

The dead body was the first thing that caught Riley's eye.

It was duct-taped upright to a post, so mangled that it hardly seemed human anymore. Tire chains were wrapped around its neck.

Hatcher's weapon of choice, Riley remembered.

"That's got to be Moran," Newton said.

Riley and Bill exchanged glances. They knew not to holster their weapons—not yet. The body might well be Hatcher's ruse to lure them into the open.

As they approached the dead man, Newton hung back, rifle ready.

Freezing pools of blood stuck to the soles of Riley's shoes as she approached the body. The face was beaten beyond all possibility of recognition, and DNA or dental records would have to be used to identify it. But Riley had no doubt that Newton was right; it must be Smokey Moran. Grotesquely, his eyes were still wide open, and the head was taped to the post so that he seemed to be staring directly at Riley.

Riley looked around again.

"Hatcher's not here," she said, holstering her weapon.

Bill did the same and walked up to the body beside Riley. Newton remained watchful, holding his rifle ready and turning to keep check on all directions.

"What's this?" Bill said, pointing to a folded piece of paper poking out of the victim's jacket pocket.

Riley took out the piece of paper. Upon it was written:

"A horse is on a 24 foot chain and eats an apple that is 26 feet away. How did the horse get to the apple?"

Riley tensed. It came as no surprise at all that Shane Hatcher had left behind a riddle. She handed the paper to Bill. Bill read it, then looked at Riley with a puzzled expression.

"The chain isn't attached to anything," Riley said.

Bill nodded. Riley knew that he understood the riddle's meaning:

Shane the Chain was now unbound.

And he was just starting to enjoy his freedom.

CHAPTER EIGHT

Sitting with Bill in the hotel bar that night, Riley couldn't get the image of the mangled man out of her head. Neither she nor Bill had been able to make sense of what had happened. She couldn't believe that Shane Hatcher had broken out of Sing Sing just to kill Smokey Moran. But there was no doubt that he had killed the man.

The bar's holiday lights seemed garish rather than a sign of celebration.

She held her empty glass out to a passing bartender. "I'll have another," she told her, handing over the glass.

Riley saw that Bill was looking at her uneasily. She understood why. This was Riley's second bourbon on the rocks. Bill knew that Riley's history with booze wasn't altogether pretty.

"Don't worry," she told him. "I'll make this my last for tonight."

She had no desire to get drunk tonight. All she wanted was to relax a little. The first glass hadn't helped, and she doubted that the second would either.

Riley and Bill had spent the rest of that day dealing with the aftermath of Smokey Moran's murder. While she and Bill had worked with local cops and the medical examiner's team at the crime scene, they'd sent Agents McGill and Newton back to the apartment building where Moran had lived. They were supposed to talk to the young gangbangers who had been standing guard in the foyer. But those young men were nowhere to be found. Moran's apartment remained unlocked and unprotected.

As the bartender set the fresh drink down in front of Riley, Riley remembered what the gangbangers had said in the foyer:

"Smokey said he thought you'd come."

"He told us to give you a message."

Then they'd told them where to find Smokey Moran.

Riley shook her head as she mentally replayed the moment.

"We should have talked to those punks when we had a chance," she told Bill. "We should have asked questions."

Bill shrugged.

"About what?" he asked. "What could they have told us?"

Riley didn't reply. The truth was, she didn't know. But the whole thing seemed strange. She remembered the gangbangers' expressions—stern, somber, even sad. It was almost as if they understood that their leader had gone to his death, and they were mourning already. The fact that they had now left their posts, apparently for good, seemed to confirm that.

So what had Moran told them before he'd left? That he wouldn't be coming back? Riley was puzzled by that possibility. Why wouldn't a smart, hardened career thug like Moran have steered clear of danger? Why did he go to that warehouse at all, if he had any idea of what awaited him there?

Interrupting Riley's thoughts, Bill asked, "What do you think will be Hatcher's next move?"

"I don't know," Riley said.

It was hard to admit, but it was true. Seasoned FBI agents were now guarding Kelsey Sprigge's house in case she was Hatcher's next target. But Riley didn't think she would be. Kelsey was right. Hatcher wouldn't kill the woman for just having done her job all those years ago, especially since she'd actually saved his life.

"Do you think he might come for you next?" Bill said.

"I wish he would," Riley said.

Bill looked a little shocked.

"You don't mean that," he said.

"I do mean that," Riley said. "If he'd only show himself, maybe I could do something. This is like playing a chess game blindfolded. How can I make my own move if I don't know his moves?"

Bill and Riley sipped on their drinks in silence for a few moments.

"You met him too, Bill," Riley said. "What's your take on him?"

Bill let out a long sigh.

"Well, he certainly seemed to figure *me* out in a hurry," he said. "He told me to forget about fixing things up with Maggie. I had no idea how right he was."

"How are things with Maggie these days?" Riley asked.

Bill rattled the ice around in his glass.

"Nowhere," he said. "I'm feeling stranded. Six months of separation, no chance of getting back together, but six months to go before the divorce becomes final. It feels like my life is standing still. At least she's easing up on custody of the boys. She's letting them spend time with me."

"That's good," Riley said.

She noticed that Bill was now gazing at her wistfully.

That's not good, she thought.

She and Bill had spent years struggling with their mutual attraction, sometimes very clumsily. Riley still winced as she remembered once drunkenly calling him and proposing that they have an affair. Their friendship and professional relationship had barely survived that miserable episode.

She didn't want to start down that road again, especially now that things were so confusing with both Ryan and Blaine. She gulped down the rest of her drink.

"It's time for me to turn in," she said.

"Yeah, me too," Bill said with a note of reluctance in his voice.

They paid the bill and left the bar. Bill headed straight toward his hotel room. In all the day's hectic confusion, Riley hadn't yet brought in her own travel bag and personal items from the car. She walked down a stairwell and through a door that led directly into the hotel's basement parking garage.

A cold blast of air hit her hard when she stepped into the concrete space. No one was in sight.

She headed straight toward the borrowed FBI SUV on the opposite side of the garage. The moment she got there and reached for the door handle, her peripheral vision caught a flash of movement somewhere to her left.

She turned her head to look. She saw nothing except parked cars, although she thought her ears detected an echo of movement. She was sure her eyes weren't playing tricks on her. Someone else was in the garage.

"Hello," she called out.

Her voice resonated loudly through the garage, followed by the moaning sound of cold wind.

A rush of adrenaline shot through her. She was sure someone was here and avoiding her sight. Who could it possibly be except Shane Hatcher?

She drew her weapon, wondering whether he had a gun as well. If so, would he use it? No, simply shooting somebody hardly seemed Hatcher's style. She wouldn't be surprised if he wasn't even armed—but he'd be no less dangerous even so.

She walked cautiously toward where she thought she'd heard the sound. Now her own footsteps sounded positively deafening as they rang through the garage. Before she'd walked more than a few feet, she heard a noisy crack behind her, followed by a rattling sound.

She whirled around, her gun raised and ready. But at that very second, she heard a clatter of running footsteps from the opposite direction. She whirled again, but saw and heard nothing.

She instantly understood what had just happened. He'd thrown something—a pebble, maybe—across the way to distract her. Now he was moving among the parked cars somewhere. But where?

Turning around and around as she walked, she threaded her way among the parked cars, looking everywhere she possibly could.

Finally she reached the garage exit. Snow was falling outside. And there he was—unmistakably silhouetted in the open space against the glaring outdoor lights.

"Hatcher!" Riley yelled, pointing her gun. "Freeze!"

She heard a familiar, grim chuckle. Then he disappeared into the night.

Riley broke into a run and rushed through the wide exit. The wind and cold were much sharper outside the garage, and Riley wasn't warmly dressed. She shivered deeply and almost choked on the cold air. Snowflakes stuck to her face and stung her skin.

The driveway outside the garage wound a short way to the well-lighted street. Turning and turning, looking everywhere, Riley called out.

"Hatcher! Show yourself!"

Now the air was filled with the low rumble of nearby traffic. Looking around at the snow-covered shapes of trees and bushes, Riley found it hard to imagine that he was hidden among them.

"Hatcher!" she yelled again.

Finally she reached the street and looked up and down the cleared sidewalks along the street. She saw no sign of anyone.

He's gone, she decided.

Still watching all sides, Riley made her way back to the garage. Just as she stepped into the broad opening, she heard a flutter of movement.

Before she could react, she was seized violently from behind.

CHAPTER NINE

The gun flew from Riley's hand as Hatcher's arm closed around her neck. She heard her weapon clatter to the concrete floor some distance away.

Hatcher's left arm was crooked around her throat, and his right forearm was braced behind her neck. It was a familiar headlock. Riley had escaped from dozens of these over the years. She seized the front arm with both hands to keep it from tightening. She knew she needed to tuck her chin, creating wriggle room for escape. But Hatcher's grip was like an iron vise, and her head was completely immobile. He was also holding her so that her feet barely touched the icy ground. She couldn't land a good backward kick.

She started to grow dizzy. His arm was crooked cannily so that it didn't completely block her windpipe. Although she was gagging, she could still breathe. But the grip cut into the flow of her carotid arteries. She realized that he was applying a calculated amount of pressure, not enough to render her unconscious but enough to disorient her.

"I guess you've got a few questions for me," he murmured softly in her ear. "Like maybe, what happened to Smokey Moran. Well, it wasn't murder. It wasn't self-defense either. It was a good old-fashioned duel."

As if he could feel the waxing and waning of Riley's consciousness, Hatcher relaxed his grip enough to give her a little more precious blood flow. He obviously wanted her to hear every word that he had to say.

"I sent him a message when I got out," Hatcher said. "I put the word out through his minions it was time for us to set our books straight. Told him the time and place and the choice of weapons—tire chains, of course."

Hatcher chuckled grimly.

"Poor bastard," he murmured. "His conscience has been eating him up for decades about the way he ratted me out like that. You know, I don't think he wanted to live with it anymore. He showed up, and we fought, and … well, you've got a pretty good idea of the rest of it. He didn't stand a chance and he knew it. The first really honorable thing Moran ever did in his life—and the last."

Now things were starting to make sense to Riley. Smokey Moran had, in fact, told his gangbanger guards that he was probably going away to his death. With Hatcher on the loose, he'd also been pretty sure that the authorities would soon show up at his

44

appointment building. So he'd ordered his taciturn but despairing followers to pass along the news.

She felt the crook of Hatcher's arm tighten. Had he finished telling her what he had to say? Was he finally going to plunge her into unconsciousness?

Her whole head buzzed and tingled and the world started to go black. She felt herself falling away from him, suddenly released from his grip. She hit the icy concrete flat on her face.

As blood started to flow back into her head, she could see where her gun had fallen, some twenty feet away from her inside the garage. She dragged herself to her feet, hoping to run and grab it.

She heard Hatcher's voice behind her.

"You don't want to do that."

She whirled around. He was standing outside in the snow. She was in the entrance, exactly midway between him and the gun.

"You don't want to do that," Hatcher repeated.

Riley's head was swimming. She could barely stay on her feet, much less think straight. Somehow, though, she vaguely realized that Hatcher was right. She didn't want to make a dash for the gun.

Why? she wondered.

Perhaps it was because she knew it would be futile. As nimble as he was strong, Hatcher would be gone before she could get her hands on the weapon.

Or maybe there was another reason—one that she didn't want to think about.

Her voice still rasping from Hatcher's chokehold, Riley said, "You killed Moran. You did what you set out to do. What now? Where do you go? What do you do?"

Hatcher took a couple of steps back into the snow, silhouetted again.

"Do you think I escaped on his account?" he said with a low laugh. "Sure, I had some unfinished business with him. But do you really think I went to the trouble of breaking out of Sing Sing because of that? He wasn't worth it."

"So why did you do it?"

Hatcher stretched out his arms in what almost seemed a generous gesture.

"Why, I did it for you, Riley," he said. "I'm here for you. And you need me right now. You need me more than anyone in the world."

"I don't understand."

"Do you remember Orin Rhodes?"

Still foggy, Riley reached back into her memory. Yes, the name was familiar. Orin Rhodes had been a killer—one of her first cases. She remembered that it had been in New York state and he'd been sent to Sing Sing for his crimes. But other details wouldn't come into focus for her. She only knew that the case had left her with some dark and ugly feelings.

"What about him?" Riley asked.

"He just got released. Early, for good behavior. A model prisoner, they said. But I know better. He got to know me—because I knew you, he said. He asked me all kinds of questions. I didn't give him any answers. He told me that he'd have his revenge. He told me it was going to be ugly. He's spent all his years looking forward to it."

Hatcher fell quiet for a moment. The snow swirled around his shadowy form with an eerie whistle.

"I couldn't let that happen," he said. "I had actually planned to take him out right there in Sing Sing. That kind of thing is possible. But then he got released early. That caught me by surprise and I had to change my plans."

He shrugged and shuffled a little.

"Besides, I'd been in there too long," he said. "Was getting lazy. This will be a lot more interesting. Ever since I met you, I've admired your mind. I've wanted to work with you. And now you've got no choice but to work with me. Believe me, this is a dangerous man, and you'll need me to stop him. You don't have a choice."

He took one menacing step toward her.

"Don't get me wrong, though," he said. "I don't care about anything or anybody but you. The whole rest of the goddamn world is expendable as far as I'm concerned. Let them die. Let them all die."

Riley saw the lights and heard the sound of an approaching car.

"But right now you need to look after the one you left at home," Hatcher said, turning and walking away from her.

The car pulled right past him into the garage. Riley made a dash for the gun and picked it up just as the car passed by it.

She heard his voice call from somewhere out in the darkness, "We're joined at the brain, Riley Paige."

She rushed out into the snowy night.

It was no good. He was gone. She knew that she couldn't possibly catch him.

She walked back into the garage, where noisy, happy, laughing people were spilling out of the car, completely unaware of what had just happened here.

Riley was still dizzy and confused. She couldn't fully remember Orin Rhodes, except that the thought of his name made her uncomfortable. If he was really out and bent on revenge, where was he right now, and what was he doing?

She remembered Hatcher's words.

"You need to look after the one you left at home."

The words triggered a wave of panic.

April's in danger, she realized.

The warm air of the hotel hallway hit Riley hard as she rushed in from the freezing garage. She didn't stop to think about what to do next. She took out her cell phone and dialed her home phone, desperately hoping to get Gabriela or April on the line.

Instead, she heard her own voice delivering the outgoing message. At the sound of the beep, she started yelling.

"April! Gabriela! Where are you? Pick up right now if you're there!"

But no one picked up.

"Please," Riley whispered. She heard the final beep and realized no one was going to answer.

Something had to be wrong.

Riley headed toward the elevator and pushed the button. Luckily, the car was already there and waiting. She got in and pushed the button for the third floor, where Bill was staying. The car seemed to rise more slowly than usual, but at least it made no stops along the way.

She had to get Bill up. They had to fly back to Quantico right away. Riley wondered whether the snow would be a problem. But they had to go.

Meanwhile, she had two phone calls to make—one to Blaine to tell him about the possible danger next door and the other to Quantico to get somebody sent there.

She was terrified that it might already be too late.

CHAPTER TEN

Orin Rhodes stopped his car in front of the townhouse. Although the car wasn't the latest model, he was sure no one would question his right to be here in this nice part of town. He was, after all, light-haired and blue-eyed, and in prison he'd learned social skills. He knew how to mislead ordinary fools about his intentions.

He kept the engine running as he looked the house over. Lights were on inside, so somebody was up and about. He knew it wasn't Riley Paige, the agent who had killed Heidi and sent him away to prison sixteen years ago. Media reports had said the FBI was investigating the escape of Shane Hatcher in Syracuse. He was sure that Riley would be there. He was also sure about who was inside the house.

Her daughter, he thought.

From years of following Paige's life and career, he knew that she had a daughter named April. She was fifteen years old, the same age that Heidi had been when Riley Paige murdered her.

April would suit his purposes perfectly, at least for now. He wasn't ready to kill Paige yet. That was going to take a lot of preparation, a lot of time spent honing a different set of skills. Meanwhile, he wanted to make her suffer, the same as he had suffered because of her. He'd passed too many years being patient and careful not to make the most of Paige's misery.

Killing her will be icing on the cake, he thought with a smile.

Meanwhile, this first attack seemed almost too easy. Breaking in from the front was out of the question, though. Even this late at night, people might be looking out windows or even coming and going from other houses.

Maybe he could just walk up to the house and ring the bell, then talk his way inside. Despite the hour, he could probably charm the girl into letting him in. He was good at that kind of thing. For almost half of his life now, he'd been wearing a mask of kindness and goodwill. That was how he'd gotten early release from prison. He'd fooled absolutely everybody—except himself.

But ringing the bell would be too risky. He didn't want to take the chance that the girl would call the cops instead of opening the door. No, the best thing was to proceed with the attack as he'd originally planned it.

He drove the car to the end of the block, turned right, then turned right again into the alley that stretched behind the row of houses. The alleyway was lined with high fences on both sides, making it impossible to see into the yards or the main floors of the houses. But each house number was painted on a back gate. Those gates would be locked, but that wouldn't be a problem.

He stopped his car at the gate behind Paige's house. This time he turned the engine off. He opened the laptop computer he'd bought just yesterday. He congratulated himself on learning all about computers while in prison. Of course, he hadn't learned the skills he needed right now in one of Sing Sing's ordinary classes. He'd been privately trained by a hacker doing prison time.

He fiddled with the computer, using the software-defined radio monitor to check for signals. As he'd expected, the house did have a wireless security system. He could see its signal on the screen. If that signal wasn't encrypted, he could send his own commands to the main controls. It would keep the system unaware of opened doors or windows until his computer battery weakened. That would give him all the time he needed.

When he had everything set to his satisfaction, Orin got out of the car and locked it, leaving the computer inside. He wasn't worried about being seen. The alley was dimly lit and no one was in sight.

He froze for a moment at a clattering sound coming from behind one of the fences. He quickly realized that it was just someone emptying garbage into a bin on the other side. The sound stopped. After a few moments, he felt sure that the person had returned to the house.

He climbed up on top of the car. He didn't much mind if he scratched or dented the clunker he'd bought as soon as he'd gotten out of prison. From the car roof, he grabbed the top of the fence with both gloved hands, then nimbly vaulted over, dropping into a crouch on the other side.

Orin took a quick look around. He saw that he had two options. Stairs led from the yard to a deck on the main floor of the house. That was where the lights were on. Beneath the deck he saw an entrance to a basement. He didn't know whether anyone might be down there, or whether the door leading up into the main house would be locked.

Then he heard faint music coming from the lighted rooms. He grinned with satisfaction. The kid must be there, where he could get to her easily. There was no reason to make his way up through the basement. He'd go directly to her.

He worked his way very quietly up the stairs. Step by step he crossed the deck. He saw that the windowed doors leading inside would be easy to open. He just had to break a pane and reach inside to turn the latch. That's when he would find out whether his interception of signals had worked. If the security alarms went off, he'd escape the way he had come.

He looked in through the door. He could see through the dining room into the living room. And he could see the girl. She was wearing pajamas and dancing.

Orin Rhodes laughed softly.

It was time to make his move.

CHAPTER ELEVEN

April hummed along with the melody as she danced. The words to the song were in Korean, so she didn't know what it was all about. But she didn't really care, either.

It felt good to be up late, to be alone, to be able to do whatever she pleased. Gabriela was downstairs, probably asleep. In any case, Gabriela wouldn't demand that April quit and go to bed. After all, April wasn't even breaking any rules or doing anything wrong. School was out for Christmas break and Gabriela would be glad that she was having fun. Things had been too serious for much too long.

She heard a faint sound, like glass breaking. She whirled around to see if she had knocked something over. Instead, she saw the back door burst open, and a man was charging toward her.

She only saw him for a blurred split-second—just long enough to see that he was small, slender, and very fast. She let out a scream, or at least the beginning of a scream. Before she could finish it, he crashed into her, knocking the wind out of her.

She immediately felt how strong he was. As she tried to resist, he threw her down and pinned her to the floor. He was on top of her, holding both of her arms down. He wasn't heavy, but he was wiry and filled with overwhelming energy.

For a moment, she was paralyzed with pure shock. She stared up at him, mesmerized by his hard blue eyes.

"Like dancing, do you?" he hissed. "We're going to do some dancing now. It'll be your last dance."

He leaned forward and kissed her on the forehead. The cold touch of his lips released her from her paralysis, and she screeched and kicked. But he was strong and held her in place.

She heard a familiar voice shout out, *"¡Diablo!"*

April saw that Gabriela was at the top of the basement stairs. She was punching numbers into her cell phone.

In a flash, the man was on his feet. He charged at Gabriela, snatched the cell phone from her hand, and threw it across the floor. He struck her hard across the face. Gabriela sagged, but held onto the stair railing. Then he kicked her in the stomach, and with a cry she fell backward down the spiral staircase.

April had regained her feet. She was now panicked about Gabriela and wanted to rush to her aid. But the man stood in her way. She whirled around and dashed away toward the front door, despite feeling ashamed of her cowardice. Just as she reached the door she heard the phone ring, and the sound of her mother's outgoing message.

She turned the deadbolt and released the chain and yanked the door open. Before she could run outside, she felt the attacker's hand seize her arm with bruising force. He jerked her back and sent her sliding across the living room floor and pushed the door shut again. Before April could regain her feet this time, he was upon her again, grabbing her by one ankle and climbing over her body.

She heard the phone beep, followed by her mother's panic-stricken voice.

"April! Gabriela! Where are you? Pick up right now if you're there!"

There was no way for April to get to the phone. Struggling to subdue her sheer animal panic, she thought hard and fast about what to do. She kicked out with her free foot and heard the attacker grunt as she struck solid flesh. The grip on her ankle loosened, and she pulled herself free.

On her hands and knees now, she reached a floor lamp and toppled it onto her assailant. Any hope that she might have hurt him vanished with the sound of his laughter.

"You've got some spunk!" he said. "Mommy must be proud of you!"

Crawling frantically, she scrambled away into the dining room. She grabbed hold of the legs of a chair, then with all her might slung it at the man behind her. He deflected it as if it were a feather and grabbed hold of her waist from behind.

April screamed and squirmed and twisted, beating him with her fists. Suddenly another man appeared behind him. April felt a surge of horror.

He's got a partner! she thought.

She knew she didn't stand a chance against two attackers.

But she quickly saw that the newcomer was Blaine Hildreth, their next-door neighbor. He had come in through the front door, which hadn't been pushed completely shut. He rushed forward and reached down and pulled her assailant off of her.

April struggled to her feet as Blaine fought with her attacker. Blaine was the taller of the two, but April immediately noticed how clumsy he seemed by comparison. He obviously wasn't accustomed to hand-to-hand fighting.

Knowing that she needed a weapon, April rushed to the fireplace and grabbed an iron poker. When she turned back toward the fray, she saw the attacker land an especially brutal blow to the middle of Blaine's abdomen. April heard Blaine let out an agonized gasp as the air burst from his lungs. He fell sharply to his knees, grasping his chest. The attacker seized his opportunity and delivered a swift kick to Blaine's head, flinging him backward to the floor. The attacker stood over Blaine, who remained silent and still. April didn't know whether he was dead or alive.

For just a moment, her path to the front door was clear. But she remembered the shame she'd felt when she'd tried to escape before. This time she was determined not to run—especially now that she had a weapon.

She rushed at her attacker and brought the poker down on his head. He was deft and quick, but even so the blow caught him on the side of the head. He staggered backward.

With all her strength, April took another swing. This time the poker caught him across the shoulder, and he reeled backward again.

But even that blow didn't stop him.

The man staggered, but then just stood glaring at her. Then he gave a wild laugh. She saw that he was enjoying this fight.

He charged at her again, his expression one of crazed glee. He struck her across the face, and she fell to her knees.

April's panic welled up and almost overcame her. Desperately, she used both hands to swing the poker upward.

It caught him in the chest. She heard him make a strange gurgling sound as he fell to the floor. He lay there, eyes closed, not moving.

April struggled to her feet. Her heart was pounding painfully, and her breathing came in huge gasps. Her attacker lay still.

Even so, she had to be sure. She raised the poker high above her head with both hands, and with all her might, brought it down on the top of his head.

Blood sprayed and his body flinched, and then he lay still.

Deathly still.

I've killed him, she thought.

Just then, she heard the sirens. April gasped in relief as the sound outside announced the arrival of police cars. She was sure that her mother had called them.

She hurried to the front door and pushed it open wide.

Then she heard a sound behind her and turned to look.

She felt a chill of terror.

He was gone.

The man she thought she had killed was gone.

She didn't know how it was possible.

The only other person in the room was Blaine, writhing on the floor. At least he was also still alive.

Then, as the police cars pulled up outside, April suddenly remembered Gabriela. In renewed panic, she hurried down the stairs. Gabriela was unconscious but breathing. Not knowing what bones might be broken, April didn't dare try to move her.

She heard a voice upstairs.

"Call an ambulance. We've got a man down."

Another voice called out, "This is the police! Is anybody here?"

April dashed up the stairs. Three cops had come in. Two had their weapons drawn, and the other was crouched beside Blaine, who was groaning now.

"I'm here," she said breathlessly to the cops. "There's a woman hurt downstairs. Please help her!"

One of the cops hurried past April and headed downstairs. Two more cops came in through the front. The female cop who was tending to Blaine turned toward April.

"What happened to the intruder?" she asked.

"He must have got out through the back," April said, pointing.

The cop yelled at the two new arrivals, "Willis, Jameson, go after him."

As the cops rushed outside, the female cop asked April, "What did you do?"

April picked up the fireplace poker, which was now lying on the floor.

"I hit him with this," she said, hardly believing her own words.

The female cop's eyes widened with surprise. She nodded with admiration.

"Good," she said.

Little by little, it started to dawn on April that she'd done something truly amazing. She was still too badly shaken for real pride to kick in.

The two cops who had gone out through the back door returned.

"The yard's clear," said one.

"So is the alley," said the other. "He got away."

The woman cop was now looking at April with a worried expression.

"Girl, I think you'd better sit down," she said.

April opened her mouth to ask why. But before the word came out, she fainted.

*

As Orin drove out of the alley in a rage, he could see the lights of the police cars flashing from the street. His breath was still coming in raspy gasps. Getting back across the fence and into his car had called on all his determination.

"The little bitch," he muttered, still hunched over in pain, still holding his bleeding scalp, the wound stinging. He checked the rearview and was relieved that at least the wound was hidden in his hairline and would not affect his appearance.

She had thought she'd killed him, and had lost her chance to really do it. What a fool she was. Hadn't she any idea that he could withstand pain a thousand times beyond that?

Now he was really angry with himself. How could he have let a child like that get the best of him?

Some revenge, he thought.

He made a sharp turn down a street that took him directly away from the scene of his disaster. As unnerved and unsettled as he was, he still had the presence of mind not to drive over the speed limit. He mustn't give cops any reason to pull him over—especially not now.

He didn't think that she had ruptured anything in his body, but he was in considerable pain. He could also feel a little blood trickling down the side of his head.

He forced himself to ignore all of it.

What mattered now was collecting his wits and his resources and getting back to his purpose. And if anything, he felt more bitterness than he had before. He'd use that anger. It would fuel his vengeance and direct his actions from now on. It would make his desire for revenge burn brighter and hotter.

"Riley Paige has no idea what she's in for," he hissed aloud.

CHAPTER TWELVE

Riley kept the siren and lights going and she raced from Quantico to Fredericksburg. In Syracuse, the snow had let up enough that the FBI pilot agreed to fly back. Here in Virginia, the night was bright and the roads were clear. Although traffic was light, she didn't want anything to slow her down. April, Gabriela, and Blaine were all in Brewster Memorial Hospital. Riley couldn't get there soon enough for her liking.

She'd just started getting the story of all that had happened and now Bill was in the passenger seat helping her with directions.

"They told you that April is all right?" Bill asked.

"They wouldn't tell me much about her," Riley said. "It sounds like Gabriela got a concussion. They're still checking for internal injuries. And as for Blaine—"

Riley couldn't finish the sentence. From what she'd heard, Blaine had gotten the worst of it. Just how bad that was she didn't yet know.

"Riley, you can't blame yourself about Blaine," Bill said. "He chose to walk in there and do what he did. It's not your fault he's not a trained lawman."

"Yeah, well," Riley said, "it's not his fault he's my neighbor, either. It sounds like he might have saved April's life. But that's my job. He never signed up for it. He never asked for it."

It troubled her that both Blaine and Gabriela had become victims. But in her heart she was most worried about April.

"Bill, what am I going to do?" she asked. "I mean, what kind of mother am I, bringing this kind of danger home with me? And don't try to tell me *that's* not my fault."

"Well, it's not," Bill said.

Riley shook her head doubtfully. Whether it was her fault or not, this was the third time that April had been victimized. First she had been kidnapped from her own father's home and held in a cage by Peterson. She'd barely gotten over the PTSD from that experience when her boyfriend had drugged her and tried to pimp her. Now this. How much more trauma could a teenage girl take?

"Something's got to change, Bill," Riley said. "Maybe it's time for me to get out of this line of work."

"This is no time to decide that," Bill said. "You're just going to have to deal with things one problem at a time."

Riley didn't reply. But she knew he was right. And one of the first items on her list was to get a new home security system installed. She'd had no idea that the one she had could fail so badly.

When they walked into the hospital emergency room, Riley was surprised by all the frenzied activity even at this hour of the morning. Ambulance teams were bringing in new patients from various places. The loudspeaker announced impending arrivals. Female and male nurses rushed about. It was a stern reminder that suffering and catastrophe never slept.

Riley and Bill hurried to the reception booth. Riley's voice shook a little as she spoke to the two nurses on duty inside.

"I'm here to see my daughter, April Paige," she said. "I'm her mother."

The two nurses looked at Riley with interest. Riley guessed that they'd heard about all that had happened. Even in a place where ongoing emergencies were the norm, this one really stood out for them.

"I'll take you to her," one of the nurses said.

The nurse led Bill and Riley to a curtained cubicle where April was lying in a bed. Her hospital gown revealed large bruises on her arms. Ryan was sitting there holding his daughter's hand. Riley was glad to see that Lucy Vargas was standing nearby.

Riley rushed over and threw her arms around April, taking care not to squeeze too hard.

Lucy told Riley, "The doctor is checking her x-rays, but it looks like cuts and bruises are the worst of it. They said that you might be able to check her out of here soon."

April pushed Riley away.

"Where were you, Mom?" she snapped angrily. "I was attacked. I was scared to death. I needed you."

"I'm sorry," Riley said, choking back a guilty sob.

Then she saw the anger vanish from April's eyes. April suddenly hugged her mother.

"It really wasn't your fault, Mom," she said, crying.

Riley held onto to April as tightly as she dared. She wondered how many times she'd have to be told things weren't her fault until she finally believed it.

Maybe never, she thought.

Ryan got up from his seat so that Riley could sit down beside the bed. Then he patted her on the shoulder.

"I'm glad you could get here, Riley," he said. Riley didn't detect the slightest note of blame or anger in his voice. "Do you need my help?"

"Not right now," Riley said. "You look tired. You should go on home. I'll call you later and tell you what we're doing."

"Then I'll see you later, sweetheart," Ryan said to April. He leaned over and gave his daughter a kiss on the cheek. For a moment he looked like he might bend down and kiss Riley too. Instead he smiled and walked away.

Riley just stared after him for a moment, still surprised by his recent change of attitude.

Then she asked April, "Can you tell me what happened?"

April knitted her brow as she remembered.

"I was dancing in the living room," she said. "You know, like I do sometimes when I'm just having fun. And then there he was. He broke in from the back. And before I knew it, he was on top of me. He was trying to—"

Riley knew what April meant but couldn't bring herself to say.

April continued, "Then Gabriela came up the stairs, and he knocked her down the stairs, and I was afraid he'd killed her. I ran for the door, but he caught me, and—"

April herself looked surprised at what she started to say next.

"I don't know how it happened, but … it was like time slowed down, and with every second, I knew better and better what to do. I hit him with a lamp, then with a chair, and when Blaine came in and got hurt, I really let him have it with a fireplace poker. I thought I'd killed him. If the police hadn't come, I—"

April sat and stared for a few seconds, grasping the enormity of what she'd done.

Then she said, "I know I really would've killed him."

Then April hugged her mother again.

As she held April tight, Riley felt a great surge of unexpected emotion. It took her a moment to realize that it was pride. Somehow, despite all her failures as a mother, she'd raised a strong and resilient girl who could more than hold her own against danger.

April tugged herself away.

"Mom!" she said. "You've got to check on Gabriela! She took such a bad fall. They said she hit her head. I'm worried sick about her."

Riley asked Lucy, "Have you seen Gabriela? Can you take me to her?"

"I'm sure she's eager to see you," Lucy said. "She's over this way." As Lucy led Riley through the ER, they stepped out of the way of an ambulance team bringing in someone on an elevated stretcher. Riley was grateful that April wasn't that badly hurt. But how was Gabriela?

It was just a short distance to Gabriela's curtained cubicle. A doctor was at her side, checking her vital signs. Her face was bruised, and her head was bandaged. But she was wide awake.

Lucy left, saying, "I'll be back with April."

"Oh, *Señora* Riley," Gabriela said. "I'm so sorry."

Riley walked over to the side of her bed.

"Sorry? Good heavens, Gabriela, what have you got to be sorry for?"

A tear rolled down Gabriela's cheek.

"That it happened," she said. "I shouldn't have let it happen."

Riley sat down and took Gabriela's hand.

"There was nothing you could do," Riley said.

"But if I could just have gotten upstairs more quick, maybe I could have done something. And then he took me by surprise. I shouldn't have been surprised. I shouldn't have let him knock me down the stairs."

Riley smiled a bit sadly. Of course Gabriela had nothing to regret. But Riley could understand all too well just how she felt.

"How is the *muchacha*?" Gabriela asked.

"She's going to be just fine," Riley said.

Riley looked at the doctor, who had just finished his examination.

"How is she?" Riley asked.

The doctor looked rather surprised.

"Amazingly well," he said. "Three broken ribs and quite a few bruises seem to be the extent of her physical injuries. Of course, because of the concussion, we need to keep her for observation—"

"*¡Híjole!*" Gabriela snapped. "You are not keeping me here for anything. I am going home as soon as somebody gives me my clothes. I have work to do."

Riley smiled as the doctor gently tried to persuade Gabriela that she had to stay. He could barely make himself heard over his patient, who let him know otherwise in a mixture of English and Spanish.

She sure seems ready to go, Riley thought.

And she doubted very much that the doctor was going to win this argument.

Riley looked at her watch. It was now six-thirty in the morning. Riley wondered if both Gabriela and April might be able to go home with her in a little while.

Then, in the midst of her relief that Gabriela and April weren't badly hurt, she remembered.

Blaine!

She rushed to a nurse who was just outside the cubicle.

"Where is my neighbor—Blaine Hildreth?" she said.

"He's in intensive care," the nurse said.

"Please take me there," Riley said.

*

The nurse led Riley directly to the intensive care unit. Blaine's daughter, Crystal, was sitting outside the glass enclosure, staring into space. A woman Riley didn't know sat beside her. She appeared to be in her twenties, tall and short-haired with a strong but gentle face. Right now she looked very tired.

Crystal didn't look up when Riley approached. The poor girl seemed to be in a state of shock.

The woman rose from her chair to greet Riley.

"Are you Riley?" she asked.

"Yes."

"I'm Felicia Mazur, the assistant manager at Blaine's restaurant. Crystal called me first thing after the whole thing happened. She came here in the ambulance with her dad. I got here as soon as I could. I'll take Crystal home to stay with me and my family until her dad's better."

Crystal finally looked up at both Felicia and Riley.

"How's Dad?" she asked as if in a trance.

Riley could tell by Felicia's look that Crystal had been asking that question repeatedly for hours now.

"I keep telling you, honey, he's going to be all right," Felicia said.

Riley looked through the window. Her heart sank as she saw Blaine lying inside the ICU, completely unconscious. He had an IV in each arm and an oxygen mask, and he was hooked up to monitors.

As Riley headed for the door, Felicia gently took her by the arm.

"You can't go in there," she said.

She led Riley a short distance from Crystal.

"He's been unconscious this whole time," Felicia said. "The doctors say he'll come out of it, but they need to keep him sedated until they check the extent of his injuries. So far they've found nothing except a cracked cheekbone and some broken ribs. They've got to make sure there isn't anything more. He'll be here for a couple of days if not longer."

Riley stood staring through the window at her injured neighbor. She felt deeply grateful that Blaine had come to April's rescue, possibly saving her life. At the same time, she felt terribly guilty. She knew that she'd risk anything to protect April, including her own life. But did she have any right to put other lives at risk?

She reminded herself of what Bill had said.

"He chose to walk in there and do what he did."

The thought didn't make her feel any better. Why did Blaine have to make that kind of choice at all?

Because he's got me as a neighbor, Riley thought.

It didn't seem fair. Nothing seemed fair right now—not to April, Gabriela, Blaine, Crystal, or even to Riley herself.

She sat down on the bench beside Crystal and put her arm around her. She wished she could tell her that everything was going to be fine from now on. But she couldn't do that. The truth was, she had no idea what to expect next—especially not now that some new killer was targeting the people Riley loved most in the world.

CHAPTER THIRTEEN

The sun was up by the time April and Gabriela were released and Riley was able to drive them home from the hospital. Meanwhile, Bill and Lucy were headed to Quantico to update Meredith. As Riley parked outside her townhouse, she saw that both local cops and FBI agents were still stationed outside.

Followed by April and Gabriela, Riley went inside to find the house still a wreck. A broken floor lamp lay across the floor, and a dining room chair with broken legs was lying on its side. Blood was sprinkled on the floor here and there. It was not yet completely dry. Cold winter air whistled in through the broken pane in the back door.

"¡Ay caramba!" Gabriela said. "I've got to start fixing all this."

"You're not doing anything of the kind," Riley said. "We're getting you both packed and out of here. Neither one of you are safe here."

Both Gabriela and April stood staring at Riley. They looked exhausted and dismayed. Riley understood why. They wanted things to go right back to normal. Riley wanted that too, but it was going to take a while.

"But there are cops and agents just outside," April said.

"They're not going to be there for long," Riley said. "You both have got to get someplace safe before they're gone. Gabriela, can you go stay with your relatives in Tennessee for a while?"

"*Sí.* But for how long?"

"Until I catch this guy," Riley said. "Pack up and call a cab to take you to the bus station. Take the next bus there."

Gabriela didn't look happy about this. Riley was glad she didn't argue.

"What about me?" April said.

"You just get packed," Riley said. "I'll work that out right now."

"Can I take a shower first?" April asked.

"No."

April rolled her eyes and started to object.

Riley said, "I'm sorry, but we just don't have time. Get everything you need for at least two or three days. Now both of you, please—go start packing."

Riley hugged them both, then April went upstairs and Gabriela went downstairs to get started packing. Riley picked up the phone and dialed Meredith's office. The team chief immediately answered.

"Agent Paige! I was going to call you. Agents Jeffreys and Vargas just got here and told me all that had happened. My God! Is April OK?"

"She will be," Riley said, hoping she was telling the truth. "That's what I need to talk to you about. Agent Meredith, I need—"

But Meredith interrupted.

"Agent Paige, I know what you need. We don't want to have this conversation on the phone. I'll send an agent right over to get things underway. For the time being, I think we'd better end this conversation."

"I understand," Riley said.

They ended the call. Riley realized that Meredith wasn't being curt. He knew that Riley wanted to put April in some kind of a safe house. Of course it wasn't the kind of thing they ought to talk about on the phone.

It was a lot to expect from Meredith. Riley knew that he'd have to overcome objections from people higher up on the chain of command. Spending funds and tying up agents to keep Riley's daughter safe was likely to provoke disapproval. By his very abruptness, Meredith was promising to get it done anyway. She felt a surge of gratitude toward her gruff but fair boss.

Now there was nothing for Riley to do but wait for Gabriela and April to finish packing, and for an agent to come with an address for the safe house. Riley sat down on her couch and looked around. It was heartbreaking to see her house in such a shambles.

Riley had been assaulted and attacked in countless ways over the years. But there was always something uniquely unpleasant about having her home invaded. She'd been through it before and knew that she'd never get used to it.

She remembered how happy she, April, and Gabriela had been to find this place and call it home. They had moved in just about six months ago. Was their dream of a safe and happy home now a thing of the past?

No, Riley thought with determination. *I'm not going to let that happen.*

*

For the second time, Riley turned her car around and backtracked along the highway. She'd been watching the traffic carefully and had taken several detours.

"Where are we going, Mom?" April asked.

Riley understood her daughter's confusion. They were taking a bizarre route that seemed to be leading them nowhere.

"Someplace where you'll be safe," Riley said.

She didn't want to explain to April that she was doing her best to make sure they weren't being followed. She preferred that April didn't have one more thing to worry about. Anyway, Riley now felt sure that nobody was on her trail. She drove directly toward the address she'd been given.

She pulled into the parking lot of a little motel. It looked like most of the other motels in that slightly disagreeable area outside of town—rather old and a little too cute in design. She drove around to the back of the building and found the right room number. She parked the car, and she and April got out and walked toward the room.

A female agent was standing outside the door waiting for them. Riley could see her radioing Quantico with the news that she and April had arrived.

"I'm Agent Tara Bricker," she said. "Come on inside."

When they entered the room, Riley saw why this was a suitable place. As ordinary as it looked outside, it was part of a sturdy old cinderblock building with thick walls and solid wood doors. The windows were small and high with wire glass in them. Both the outside door and the door to the inside hallway had peepholes and security cameras.

As Riley looked the place over, Agent Bricker said, "Special Agent in Charge Meredith wants me to tell you that this place is truly safe. The Bureau has used it before, and it's owned by someone we trust. It's also got an excellent security system."

Riley saw that April was looking around with dismay at the rather shabby furnishings.

Pointing to the door connecting to the next room, Agent Bricker said, "Either I or another female agent will always be right through that door. We'll bring you food whenever you want it. I understand that you already know Agent Lucy Vargas. She's offered to spend some time here."

April's eyes were wide and her mouth hung open. She seemed to be struggling to grasp her situation.

"Can't I even go outside?" she asked.

"I'm sorry, but no," Agent Bricker said.

April sat down on the edge of the bed, looking very unhappy. Agent Bricker seemed to detect her mood.

"I'll leave the two of you to get settled in," she told April and Riley.

Then she left through the door leading into the next room. Riley sat down beside April.

"Mom, this is going to be like being in jail," April said.

Riley wished she could tell her otherwise. After all that April had just survived, it seemed horribly unfair to put her through this. She put her arm around her.

"I'm going to fix this soon," she said.

"Can you come around and visit me?"

"I'm sorry, but I can't do that. Sooner or later I might get followed."

Riley realized it was best not to drag things out. She kissed April on the cheek and got up to leave.

"Mom, don't go," April said.

"I've got to, honey."

"But why? There are lots of other agents. Why can't you just stay here with me? Let somebody else catch this guy."

Riley felt a pang of despair. She more than half wished she could do just what her daughter asked.

"April, it's my job. I've got to go."

April got up from the bed and wrapped her arms tightly around Riley.

"I'm scared," April said.

"You'll be safe here," Riley said.

"I'm not scared about me. I'm scared about you. I'm afraid you'll—"

April paused for a moment, choking on a sob.

Riley returned April's embrace.

"I'm going to be all right," she said. "I promise. Just you wait and see."

Struggling against her own tears, Riley disentangled herself from the embrace and left the room. As she got into her car, she thought about the promise she'd just made. She hoped she could keep it.

CHAPTER FOURTEEN

Riley knew that things were about to get really ugly. She and Bill were in the conference room reporting to Brent Meredith about their activities in Syracuse. She wished Special Agent in Charge Carl Walder hadn't joined the meeting.

Walder was Meredith's boss—a babyish, freckle-faced man with curly, copper-colored hair. He had risen up in the FBI food chain through deals, connections, and politics. Riley had no respect for him—nor did he have any respect for her.

Their history hadn't been pretty. Walder had fired her twice, taking away her gun and badge. As he sat across the table glaring at her, Riley knew perfectly well that he was itching for a chance to do it again—this time for good.

I might be giving him that chance any minute now, she thought.

So far, she and Bill had told Meredith and Walder about their meeting with retired Agent Kelsey Sprigge and about the body they'd found in the rundown warehouse. The two chiefs already knew about the events in Syracuse, but Riley and Bill had plenty of details to fill in.

After they'd finished describing Smokey Moran's murder, a silence fell over the room.

"Is that everything?" Walder asked.

Riley wished it was everything. They'd gotten to the part of the story she wished she could talk about without Walder there. Meredith might understand. Walder certainly wouldn't.

"As you know," Riley said cautiously, "I was warned that Orin Rhodes had been released and wanted revenge against me. I realized that April was in danger."

After a pause, she added, "I acted accordingly. I called for help and came back from Syracuse as fast as I could."

Walder leaned across the table toward Riley.

"You were warned?" he asked. "By whom?"

Riley gulped. She exchanged uneasy glances with Bill. So far, he was the only person she'd told the next part of her story.

"I was warned by Shane Hatcher," she said.

Bill drummed his fingers nervously on the table, anticipating trouble. Walder and Meredith looked surprised.

"Shane Hatcher," Walder said in a grim, tight voice. "The man you were sent to Syracuse to hunt and capture."

Riley nodded. "Yes, sir."

"He warned you."

Riley repeated, "Yes, sir."

"And how exactly did that happen?" Walder asked.

Riley took a long, slow breath. She hoped she could keep this part of her account as short and simple as possible.

"He took me by surprise in our hotel garage. He got me in a headlock that I couldn't get out of. When he released me, I couldn't get my gun. So I listened to what he had to say. He knows Orin Rhodes from Sing Sing. Rhodes told him that he was going to get even with me for putting him away."

Riley stopped short. Should she tell them the rest? That Hatcher had told her he'd escaped solely to help her and work with her, and that he was only tying up a loose end by killing Moran?

She remembered Hatcher's words.

"We're joined at the brain, Riley Paige."

She hadn't even told Bill about all of that. If she brought it up now, it would only make more trouble. And she was in plenty of trouble already.

Walder was looking at her with great suspicion.

"So you met Hatcher in a garage …" he began.

"It wasn't my idea."

"You met Hatcher in a garage," Walder repeated firmly, "and you didn't apprehend him."

"Sir, he's fast, strong, and smart. I'm sorry, but I couldn't. I don't think I've ever been up against anyone like him before."

Walder leaned back in his chair.

"You said you couldn't get your gun," he said. "Explain that to me."

Riley winced at the memory.

"It flew out of my hand when he grabbed me," she said. "I couldn't get it back until he was gone."

"So you let him go," Walder said.

"Not deliberately."

"Really?"

Walder was staring her straight in the eyes. Riley hoped he couldn't see a spasm of self-doubt there. Could she have gotten the gun back?

She remembered the moment vividly. She'd been standing in the garage entrance, midway between Hatcher and the gun. She'd thought about making the twenty-foot sprint to get the weapon back. But then Hatcher had said:

"You don't want to do that."

And she'd stopped short. It probably wouldn't have mattered otherwise. Surely if she'd made a lunge for the gun, Hatcher would have been gone before she could use it. Even so, she hadn't even tried. She'd stood spellbound listening to what he had to tell her.

Was it true? Had she not caught him because she didn't want to catch him? Was her bond with him so powerful that she subconsciously wanted him to be free?

Walder said, "You let him go, and now you're going to fix it. I expect you and Agent Jeffreys to apprehend Hatcher within forty-eight hours if not sooner."

Riley shook her head.

"I think my focus should be on catching Orin Rhodes," she said.

"Why?" Walder asked.

"Right now he's more of a threat than Hatcher."

Walder let out a gasp of disbelief.

"More of a threat? Agent Paige, in the short time since his escape Hatcher has already killed. He beat a man to death with chains."

"A man who betrayed him," Riley said.

Walder was really angry now.

"What's that supposed to be, an excuse? Does that make it all right? He also probably killed the driver of the book delivery truck he escaped in. We just haven't found the body yet. And you don't think he's much of a threat? He's just getting started."

Riley felt her own rage rising.

"Orin Rhodes tried to kill my daughter," she said, her voice shaking.

Walder slammed his fist on the table.

"Which is why I don't want you on his case. You're too emotionally involved. I'm assigning cooler heads."

Riley bit her tongue. She knew that anything she said right now would only prove Walder's point.

So would jumping across the table and throttling him, she thought.

Walder stood up.

"You blew your chance to catch Hatcher, Agent Paige." he said. "Now you're going to fix it. And you've got forty-eight hours. Remember that."

He stormed out of the room. Riley, Bill, and Meredith sat in silence for a moment.

At last Meredith spoke in a quiet voice.

"Agent Paige, your daughter's safe right now," he said. "Rhodes can't get to her. And you can't turn this into a personal vendetta."

Riley said nothing.

"Listen to me," Meredith said. "The Bureau's under tremendous pressure because of the Hatcher thing. His whole history is all over the papers and the Internet—how 'Shane the Chain' spent years becoming a brilliant criminologist, how he managed a stunning escape from Sing Sing, and how he's on the loose now settling old scores. He's the perfect Internet folk antihero—a criminal genius, admired and feared at the same time. He's already even got fan clubs. It's a hell of a mess for us. That's why Walder is being so—"

Meredith paused.

"We've got to put him away," he said. "*You've* got to put him away. You and Agent Jeffreys."

"I understand, sir," Riley said, almost in a whisper.

"Good," Meredith said. "Now I want the two of you to put together a written report of what happened in Syracuse. Get it to me before the end of the day. Tomorrow morning at seven-thirty, you're flying back to Syracuse."

Bill and Riley left the conference room. Riley sensed that Bill was worried about her.

"You haven't had much sleep," he said.

Riley didn't reply. The truth was, she hadn't had any sleep since the night before last—before they'd even gone to Syracuse.

"I'll take a crack at the report," he said. "I'll email it to you to check when I've got it drafted. You just go home and get rested."

"Thanks," Riley said.

Riley felt the need to sit down and clear her head before driving home. She went to her office and sat at her desk. She swiveled in her chair, trying to settle her nerves. She just couldn't do it. She was sure that Orin Rhodes was the true threat right now, not Hatcher. But there was no way for her to explain to her colleagues why she knew that.

In all the chaos that had ensued since yesterday, she hadn't had time to think about Orin Rhodes and why he had targeted her for revenge. She got up from her desk, went to the filing cabinet, and pulled out a yellowed, sixteen-year-old folder filled with information about the case. It was her personal file, one she had kept even after the materials had been scanned and entered into the FBI database. She spread out the photos and reports on her desk.

The first images to catch her eye were mugshots of Orin Rhodes. It had been about sixteen years since she'd seen that face. She'd forgotten how young he'd been when she'd brought him to justice—only seventeen years old, and he looked even younger.

Looking at the picture, she hardly saw the face of a hardened killer. But the boy looked troubled and sullen.

Skimming through the case history, she was reminded that Orin had come from a broken home in Hinton, New York. He lived part of the time with an alcoholic father and the other part with a very erratic mother. He'd dropped out of high school early. Before the murders, his prior record showed nothing worse than a little shoplifting.

Not a bad kid, Riley thought.

Or at least he'd shown no signs of being a bad kid before he'd taken to killing. He'd been just an ordinary adolescent boy who'd been dealt a bad hand in life. But in a single day, something had happened to change all that.

Before Riley could remember exactly what it had been, her eye was caught by a school photo of a very young girl. She was awkward-looking but rather pretty, and she had an empty, sad expression.

The girl's name came back to Riley with a jolt.

Heidi Wright.

It was a name that she hadn't thought about for years, a name that she'd tried to forget.

Heidi Wright was the first person Riley ever killed.

*

Riley stared at the photo of Heidi Wright in shock for a moment. Then as she started reading, the horrible event came back into her memory.

Heidi had been Orin Rhodes' girlfriend, and she'd been just fifteen years old at the time. According to Orin Rhodes' own testimony, she had called him at home one day, frantic and crying, saying she was in danger and begging him to come and save her.

Orin had picked up his father's revolver and dashed straight over to Heidi's home, just in time to find her being sexually assaulted by both her older brother and her father. Orin had shot both men dead.

The two desperate teenagers decided to go on the lam, but didn't have any money. Heidi did have her father's gun. Both of them armed, they fled her home and drove to the nearest liquor store. Their attempted holdup went bad, and they wound up shooting and killing both the manager and an employee.

That's when it seemed that their inner demons took over. The killings had given them an unexpected, euphoric rush, and they wanted to feel that again. They wanted to kill more. The two twisted kids drove to Jennings, a little town nearby, where they snatched two unsuspecting people off the street—first a man and next a teenage girl. Each time, they tormented their victim with gunplay, inflicting repeated wounds before the final execution.

That was when it became an FBI case. Riley was brought in from Quantico, along with her then-partner and mentor Jake Crivaro. It was one of Riley's first cases, and she hadn't been emotionally prepared for its outcome.

Local police and FBI agents cornered Heidi Wright and Orin Rhodes in a motel on the outskirts of Jennings. The young couple fired from their room window while cops and agents—Riley among them—shot back from behind vehicles in the parking lot.

After a few minutes of exchanged gunfire, Heidi and Orin had seemed on the verge of surrendering. But then Heidi suddenly rushed out of the room into the parking lot, her gun blazing at the cops and agents.

Riley shot her and killed her. She'd had no choice. Staggered with grief and out of bullets, Orin quietly surrendered.

Riley remembered what a sad, broken figure Orin had cut at the trial. He pleaded guilty to all charges and had seemed deeply penitent. If he had blamed Riley for Heidi's death, he'd given her no sign of it. In fact, he said that he blamed Heidi's death entirely on himself. When he'd received his life sentence, he'd nodded in what seemed like heartbroken agreement.

Riley's fingers trembled a little as she handled the old photo of Heidi, who looked like such an ordinary teenager. It dawned on her that she'd killed Heidi when the girl was almost exactly April's age. The bitter irony deepened when Riley considered that April had been born just a year after Heidi had died.

Riley's heart ached at the memory that she'd so long tried to put behind her. But forgetting was no longer possible. Orin had marked her for revenge—and April as well.

She remembered what Shane Hatcher had told her.

"He just got released. Early, for good behavior. A model prisoner."

It seemed strange. The penitent teenager she'd seen in the courtroom had appeared to live into his thirties trying to seek some kind of redemption, doing whatever good he could while in prison, blaming no one but himself for his own downfall and Heidi's death.

But now that he was free, things had changed.

Either that, Riley thought, *or things were never what they seemed.*

CHAPTER FIFTEEN

When Riley and Bill stepped off the plane at Syracuse Hancock International Airport, cold air hit her in the face like an icy blast of déjà vu. After all, they had just flown out of here the night before last.

There weren't any local agents here to meet them this time. Instead, a rental car had been reserved for them. Bill and Riley went to the airport rental desk to pick up the keys. They stepped outside the terminal and started walking to the garage where the car was parked.

Then Riley stopped.

"You drive on to the field office, Bill," she said. "I'm catching a cab. I ... want to go somewhere else first. I'll meet you there later."

Bill looked at her with surprise. He obviously wanted to ask where she wanted to go.

She looked at him with an expression that gently implored:

"Don't ask."

To her relief, Bill only nodded.

"I'll see you later," he said.

Bill walked on to the rental car. Riley dialed Kelsey Sprigge's number on her cell phone. Kelsey answered.

"Kelsey, this is Riley Paige," she said. "Some things have happened since I last talked to you."

"Oh, yes," Kelsey said. "I saw it on the news. Awful business about what happened to Smokey Moran. But then, I believe you more or less expected it, didn't you? I should have expected it too. That awful man was always sure to meet a bad end. And now Shane Hatcher's a celebrity! Where's it all going to end?"

Riley paused for a moment.

"Kelsey, I'd like to drop by and ask you a few more questions," she said.

*

A little while later, Riley was sitting beside a warm fire with Kelsey Sprigge. She'd just finished telling Kelsey about all that had happened since they'd last met, including her confrontation with Hatcher and Orin Rhodes' attack on April.

Kelsey nodded sagely when Riley finished talking.

"Yes, I remember the Orin Rhodes case," she said. "I wasn't assigned to work on that one—not allowed to, really. The men in the office were rather embarrassed that a 'girl' had brought down Shane Hatcher. So they never put me on a case like that again. Kept me doing paperwork or on boring cases. They said they were just trying to keep me out of danger. I always knew better."

Shaking her head, Kelsey added, "I'm so glad your daughter wasn't badly hurt. Your housekeeper as well. And your neighbor—I do hope he's going to be all right."

"I hope so too," Riley said.

For a moment, the only sound was the crackling from the fireplace.

"But you haven't told me why you wanted to drop by, dear," Kelsey finally said.

Riley didn't reply. The truth was, she herself wasn't at all sure why she'd come.

Kelsey gazed at Riley, her crinkly eyes full of wisdom.

"There's something you haven't told me," she said. "Something you haven't told anybody. You left it out of your report. You haven't even told your partner."

Riley smiled a little.

"How can you tell?" she asked.

Kelsey chuckled softly.

"Oh, maybe it's just a little leftover skill from my days as an agent. More likely, though, it's from all my years as a wife and mother. You learn to listen—not just to what people are saying, but also to what they're not saying."

Kelsey reached over and patted Riley on the knee.

"There's no hurry," she said. "But I think you should tell me."

Riley took a couple of long, slow breaths.

At last she said, "When I was in the garage with Hatcher, he told me exactly why he'd escaped. He said it was because of me. He admires my mind, he said. He's always wanted to work with me. And he says I need him—that I really need his help right now."

After a pause, Kelsey asked, "Is he right?"

The question cut Riley to the quick. Although she hadn't realized it, this was exactly the possibility that had been troubling her.

"He told me that we were 'joined at the brain,'" Riley said. "If that's true, what does it make me? Am I just a monster like he is?"

Kelsey sighed.

"Well, in my experience, there are lots of kinds of monsters. Take Lucien Wayles, for example—the cop Hatcher killed in such

73

an awful way. He was a good man, folks said. He'd saved people's lives, protected and served the community with honor and distinction. He was also corrupt to the core, and I'm pretty sure he was guilty of at least one murder himself."

Kelsey thought for a moment, then continued.

"And take Smokey Moran, who turned in his best friend for a 'get-out-of-jail' card, then spent the rest of his life spreading nothing but destruction and death. Wayles and Moran were monsters without a code. Shane Hatcher is a different sort of monster. He's nothing like them at all."

Kelsey sat staring at the fire for a moment before she spoke again.

"Just between you and me, dear, some monsters are worthy of respect. You don't have to like them. And it's your job to stop them and put them away, to kill them if you have to. But you still need to respect them. It's the only way to deal with them."

"Is Orin Rhodes that kind of monster?" Riley asked.

Kelsey knitted her brow in thought.

"Something happened to him that day all those years ago," she said. "His life stopped making sense, even to him. When he killed the girl's brother and father for trying to rape her—well, that still made sense. Then when he and the girl killed the liquor store owner and the employee, there was at least a reason for it. But then something happened. They killed two people for no reason at all. Why? I doubt that they even knew."

Kelsey scratched her chin thoughtfully.

"Shane Hatcher told you he wanted to help you, to work with you. Well, Shane Hatcher might be a lot of awful things, but he's a man of his word. You have every reason to believe him."

Kelsey shook her head.

"But Orin Rhodes is another story. He lost his way a long time ago. And he's never even tried to find his way back. He likes being lost. It suits him. He's got no compass, there's no rhyme or reason to what he thinks or does. He's been nursing and nurturing his rage and hatred for sixteen years now, and nobody even knew it. And now he's free to do ... God knows what."

They both sat in silence for a moment.

"Shane Hatcher is not your biggest problem right now, dear," Kelsey finally said. "And if the FBI thinks otherwise, they're wrong. But Orin Rhodes—well, he scares me, and he ought to scare you, too."

A strange mix of feelings came over Riley. She was grateful to Kelsey and glad she'd come to see her. She'd needed her insight and wisdom. And Kelsey had just confirmed what Riley's gut had been telling her.

At the same time, Riley was confused. Here she was in Upstate New York, under orders to catch or kill Shane Hatcher before two more days passed. Meanwhile, Orin Rhodes had made his most recent attack at her home in Fredericksburg. And nobody knew what direction he'd headed toward after that.

Where is he now? Riley wondered. *And what's he going to do next?*

CHAPTER SIXTEEN

Orin Rhodes stood studying his face in the mirror. He had a deep cut on his left temple where the girl had clipped him with the fireplace poker. But he didn't mind. He hadn't been recognized on account of it, and he'd gotten far enough away from Fredericksburg not to worry about it now.

He liked the face that he saw.

No more mask, he thought, touching his face all over.

It had been sixteen years since he'd seen this face—sixteen years of wearing a mask all the time.

He remembered with sour disgust his lonely life of deception in prison. His endless displays of insincere contrition. The hours he'd passed pretending to "improve" himself in classes. The many younger prisoners he'd mentored, counseling them to follow the straight and narrow. He'd even organized his own small Bible group! Never mind that he believed in precisely nothing in the world, let alone Jesus or any other higher power.

Through all those years, he'd only revealed his true face to one man—Shane Hatcher. Orin had thought he'd found a kindred spirit. But Hatcher turned his back on him, wanted nothing to do with him.

It had been a crushing disappointment.

And now he heard on the radio that Hatcher had escaped. Not that Orin much cared. "Shane the Chain" had his own agenda, one that didn't concern Orin in the least. Their paths would never cross again, he was sure of that.

He smiled at the face he now saw. He was amazed by how young he looked, as if that fateful day of his capture and Heidi's death had been only yesterday.

At last it was time to make up for all the lost years.

There's no time like the present, he thought.

He'd been in hiding for long enough.

He opened a drawer and took out his CZ P-09 pistol, loaded a nineteen-round clip into it, and put a suppressor on the muzzle. He'd spent quite a lot on this getup, and he was determined to get his money's worth out of it.

He tucked the gun under his belt, put on a warm parka, and stepped outside his rented cabin. The winter air out here in the woods was cold and bracing. He felt more energized with every passing second.

He walked along a trail toward the lake, putting some distance between himself and the cabin. When the lake came into view, he took his smartphone out of his pocket and set its countdown timer for ten minutes.

He was acting according to a plan he'd dreamed up many years ago in prison. And his plan was basically to have no plan at all.

Chance was the story of his life, after all—and of Heidi's short life as well. They hadn't planned on all that had happened to them. It wasn't their fault. If Heidi's brother and father hadn't tried to force themselves on her, Orin wouldn't have had to kill them. If the two men at the liquor store hadn't resisted, he and Heidi wouldn't have had to kill them either.

By the time they'd arrived in Jennings, they'd learned their lesson. They understood their purpose in life. And that purpose was simple—to destroy life without purpose at all, purely randomly, with no rhyme or reason.

They'd killed the man and the girl simply because they were the first people to cross their paths. If Orin and Heidi had escaped that shootout at the motel, they would have kept right on traveling across the state, killing in the most random ways they could think of until they were caught or killed. A flip of a coin might decide whether some unsuspecting person lived or died.

But they hadn't escaped. And that FBI bitch had shot Heidi dead.

He didn't imagine that Riley Paige had wanted to kill anybody. She'd gotten caught in the web of chance, just like he and Heidi had. Although Paige didn't know it, she was now hopelessly tangled in the net of his hatred.

And he hated her with every fiber of his being—hated her for nothing more than being in the wrong place at the wrong time, hated her for being the agent whose job had been to kill Heidi. After all, that was what life was all about.

Just one damn thing after another.

He'd made a terrible mistake by targeting the woman's daughter. That had been too personal, too premeditated, too planned. It was no wonder he'd failed. He'd forgotten the most important lesson of his life:

Chance is everything.

Like himself and Heidi, everybody in the world was a victim of chance. Most people didn't know that. But a man with a gun and no real purpose at all except to kill could sure teach people in a hurry.

I'll sure teach Riley Paige, he thought. *She'll come for me and it won't matter where or when she does.*

He was almost at the end of the path that led to the lake. He looked at his smartphone. Four minutes had passed. If he saw someone, anyone, in the next six minutes, he'd kill them. If not, he'd simply wait a couple of hours before going through the same procedure all over again. Whoever passed by when the clock *wasn't* running would go away unharmed, unaware of how kind chance had been to them.

Just as he stepped out of the woods onto the enormous rocks along the edge of the lake, he saw a man coming toward him along the shore. From the way he moved, Orin thought that he must be fairly old. He was carrying a lot of fishing tackle.

The man sat down on a rock by the lake and began to unpack his gear.

Orin walked toward him, smiled, and called out to him.

"A little cold for fishing, ain't it?"

Surprised, the man turned around and smiled.

"Perfect time for crappie," he said.

He started putting his fishing rod together.

Orin took his gun out of his belt, raised it, aimed, and fired. The suppressor kept the noise from echoing across the lake. Instead, the gun made a sharp crack like a large dry twig breaking, followed by the whistle of the flying bullet.

Orin could hear the bullet's thudding impact as it hit the man's shoulder. The man hunched over with a loud groan of pain. Then he turned and looked at Orin.

"What the hell?" he said.

Orin just stood there smiling, pointing the gun at him. The man scrambled to his feet and stumbled toward the woods, hoping to escape. It was exactly what Orin wanted. He fired another shot that hit the man in the thigh. He watched as his prey fell to the ground and started to scramble desperately through the brush.

Seventeen rounds left, Orin reminded himself, following him.

It was important to keep count. He was going to keep the man alive and in mounting pain until finishing him off with the very last bullet in his clip.

Just the way Heidi would have liked it, Orin thought, firing again.

CHAPTER SEVENTEEN

Riley's features were set in determination as she drove into the little town of Jennings.

"This can't be a good idea," Bill said from the seat beside her.

Riley didn't know what to say to reassure him. The truth was, she more than half agreed with him. What good was it going to do to revisit the town where she'd killed a fifteen-year-old girl all those years ago? It wasn't as if she expected Orin Rhodes to turn up here, of all places.

And of course, she was acting against Walder's explicit orders.

"I expect you and Agent Jeffreys to apprehend Hatcher within forty-eight hours if not sooner."

Time was running short. While Riley had been visiting Kelsey Sprigge, Bill had gone straight to the Syracuse field office to check on the status of the Hatcher case. He'd also returned to Smokey Moran's apartment and helped a couple of agents ransack the place in search of any clues. Not surprisingly, they'd turned up nothing. And of course, Moran's taciturn bodyguards were still nowhere to be found.

Hatcher's trail had run cold, and Riley had talked Bill into coming with her to Jennings. No, it probably was a bad idea. And it surely wasn't fair for her to drag Bill along as she sabotaged her own career. They were risking his career too.

But here they were. They'd just have to make the best of it.

Riley parked in front of a pleasant, two-story colonial house with a picket fence, a snow-filled yard, and smoke curling up out of the chimney. It was the home of Ava Strom, whose seventeen-year-old daughter Rusty had been walking to school when Orin Rhodes and Heidi Wright had abducted her. They'd taken her just outside of town and killed her slowly with many rounds of bullets.

The murderous couple had also killed a local handyman named Myron Wilder in exactly the same manner. But Wilder didn't have any surviving relatives in Jennings. Rusty did. So Riley had called on the way here to tell Ava Strom that they'd like to talk to her. The woman hadn't sounded as if she liked the idea, but she hadn't said no.

Bill and Riley walked up onto the porch and rang the doorbell. Ava Strom came to the door.

"Yes?" she said.

Riley and Bill both produced their badges. Before they could introduce themselves, Ava Strom said, "I know who you are. You told me on the phone. Come on in."

Riley and Bill stepped into the front foyer. Ava Strom did not invite them to come on into the living room, much less to sit down. She clearly wanted to keep things short.

Ava was in her fifties—an ordinary-looking woman with a strangely empty expression.

"My husband's at work," she said, crossing her arms. "He has a real estate business here in Jennings."

Ava Strom fell silent. Her silence delivered an unspoken message that her husband was not to be bothered by all this.

Riley said, "Ms. Strom, I'm sorry to bring back difficult memories. But we're here to talk to you about your daughter's murder."

"Why?"

Her glare and her sharp tone of voice brought Riley up short.

Bill said, "The truth is, Orin Rhodes was released from prison a few days ago."

Ava Strom didn't react at all.

"I heard he was a model prisoner," Ava Strom said.

"That's what everybody thought," Riley said. "But he's turned violent again."

Another silence fell. Riley got the distinct feeling that Ava Strom simply didn't care. And maybe she had no reason to care. Riley certainly had no reason to believe that she or her husband might become Orin Rhodes' targets. Still, her lack of any alarm or even interest was vaguely disconcerting.

At last Riley said, "Ms. Strom, before it happened, did you have any idea—?"

Before Riley could finish her question, Ava Strom said, "I fixed her breakfast that morning. Bacon and eggs and toast. She sat at the kitchen table and ate and had a book open to study. While she was eating I started right to work in the kitchen getting supper ready. I didn't pay any attention to her. I don't remember that either of us said a word to each other. I didn't even say goodbye when she left, and she didn't either. That was the last time I saw her."

Ava Strom looked off into space.

"I keep thinking I should have known right then. Maybe I should have done or said something. Just a word or a smile, or maybe a scolding about eating too fast, or about eating and studying at the same time, or a question about what she was going to do that day. I keep thinking something stupid like that might have changed everything. That doesn't make sense, does it?"

"No, it doesn't," Riley said.

She resisted the urge to add, *"And you're not answering the question I'm trying to ask."* By now she knew better than to expect useful answers. The woman had none to give. She was emotionally numb to the world, and had been for many years now.

Ava Strom shrugged.

"Well, there you have it," she said. "The story of our lives, Logan's and mine, ever since it happened. Nothing makes sense anymore. I don't suppose anything will really make sense ever again."

She walked to the door and opened it, letting in a cold blast of air.

"And now, if you don't mind, I'm sure I don't have anything else to tell you that would do any good," she said.

Riley nodded slowly.

"Thank you for your time, Ms. Strom," she said. "We'll leave now."

When Bill and Riley got back into the car, Bill said, "That was pointless, Riley. We didn't learn a thing. What are we doing here, anyway?"

Riley didn't reply as she started the car. She couldn't disagree. Perhaps this whole detour had simply been a bad idea.

But she knew where she wanted to go next. It was the motel where the shootout had taken place. She thought it might help to relive what happened there—this time trying to imagine things from Orin Rhodes' point of view. As she often did when visiting crime scenes, maybe she could get inside his skin, finally make some sense of him.

As she drove through town, she noticed how different everything looked from when she'd been here all those years ago. Once a quaint and simple colonial-era town, it was now gentrified. Even the older houses and buildings had lost their charm through remodeling.

She found the address she was looking for. For a moment she thought she must have come to the wrong place. There was no motel anymore. Instead, there was a rather tacky pseudo-colonial strip mall.

She stopped the car in the large parking lot.

"Give me just a minute," she said to Bill.

She got out of the car and walked around alone, trying to get her bearings, trying to imagine the place as it used to be. But it was impossible to do. It was as if the whole incident, including Heidi Wright's death and Orin Rhodes' arrest, had been bulldozed clean off the face of the earth.

A bitter irony was starting to sink in.

The interview had been meaningless. And now even this place was meaningless too. It was as if she were getting her nosed rubbed in the meaninglessness of it all.

Maybe that's the point, she thought.

Maybe it was time for her to stop expecting anything about this case to make sense. Maybe she couldn't bring Orin Rhodes back to justice unless she abdicated any hope of making sense of him. That was likely to be hard to do. It went against every instinct she had as an agent.

Before she could turn to walk back to the car, her cell phone rang. She didn't recognize the number of the caller. But as she answered, she heard a familiar voice.

"Bet you were wondering when you'd hear from me again."

It was Shane Hatcher. The next thing he said was, "Don't bother trying to trace. This is a burner phone, and anyhow, I'll be long gone."

"Where are you?" Riley asked. "Are you somewhere nearby?"

"Not if you're in Jennings. That's where I'd expect you to be. Or else you've already been there, or you're planning to go there soon. But I think that's where you are right now. Am I right?"

Riley didn't reply. Hatcher chuckled, obviously taking her silence for a yes.

"You shouldn't be so predictable, Riley. Especially when dealing with this guy. Believe me, he's anything but predictable. No, I'm a long way from Jennings, and so is he."

Riley's mind raced as she tried to process the hints that Hatcher was giving her.

"You've been tracking him, haven't you?" Riley asked. "Are you in Fredericksburg? Are you anywhere near April? Is he anywhere near her?"

Riley heard a snort of laughter.

"What do you think?"

She made no reply.

"What do you think?" he asked again, more insistently. "Is he going after April again right now?"

"No," Riley said, starting to understand his meaning.

"Why not?"

"It makes too much sense."

Hatcher let out a chuckle of hearty approval.

"Has he killed anybody else?" Riley asked.

She heard a sigh of impatience.

"Riley, Riley, Riley. What did I say to you back in that garage? I don't care who he kills. I only care about you. And you're falling way behind."

Without another word, Hatcher ended the call.

Standing there dumbly in the cold, Riley suddenly knew:

He's killed already. And I have no idea where, how, or who.

CHAPTER EIGHTEEN

Riley could see that Brent Meredith was in a bad mood. She and Bill had just flown back to Quantico from Syracuse and sat down for a meeting in the team chief's office. She noticed Meredith checking his watch, but she waited for him to begin the conversation.

"Agents Paige and Jeffreys," Meredith said, "Walder gave you a forty-eight-hour deadline to catch Hatcher. Your time runs out in eighteen hours. What are your chances?"

"Not good, sir," Bill said. "Hatcher's not in Syracuse. That much we're sure of."

"And you didn't pick up a single new clue?" Meredith asked.

Riley glanced at Bill. He nodded, indicating that she'd better tell Meredith the truth.

"Not exactly a clue, sir," she said. "But he called me."

Meredith's eyes widened. Riley was really glad that Walder wasn't here. Fortunately, coming in this late wasn't his style. This was going to be hard enough to explain to Meredith.

"Called you?" Meredith said. "And this is the first I'm hearing about it?"

"He called on a burner phone, impossible to trace," Riley said. "There was no point in reporting it at the time."

Meredith put his feet up on his desk in a mock-casual manner.

"Well, Agent Paige—is there anything you'd like to share with me about your little chat? Or was your conversation of a purely personal nature?"

Riley felt stung. She mentally weighed what to say. She figured it was probably just as well not to mention that she and Bill had taken a little detour to Jennings. If Bill chose to say something about it, he could do so. But given Meredith's sour disposition, it seemed best to stick to just part of the facts for now.

"He seems to be tracking Orin Rhodes," Riley said. "He gave me the distinct impression that Rhodes has killed someone. Who, why, or where, I've got no idea."

Meredith looked puzzled and far from pleased.

"Do you believe him?" he said.

"I do, sir," Riley said.

"Why?"

The question brought Riley up short. She didn't say anything.

Meredith said, "Agent Paige, this is the second time you've been contacted by the man you're supposed to bring to justice. And you're nowhere near apprehending him. Just what the hell is going on? Why is he staying in touch with you?"

Riley felt more and more fortunate that Walder wasn't here to throw a fit about things. Meredith was being tough enough.

And it wasn't an easy question to answer. So far she'd only told Kelsey Sprigge the real reason for Hatcher's escape. He'd done it for Riley, because he admired her and wanted to help her—or so he said, and Riley had no reason not to believe him. But she couldn't bring herself to say that even to Bill, let alone to Meredith. She wasn't sure why, except that her whole connection with Hatcher terrified her somehow.

"He knows me, sir," Riley said.

Meredith sat quietly thinking for a moment.

"I'm going to have to sort all this out with Walder tomorrow morning," he said. "Agent Jeffreys, I'll want you to be at our meeting. Agent Paige, I think maybe you should stay clear of the BAU at least until tomorrow afternoon. I've got a feeling you'd better not cross Walder's path right now."

"Yes, sir," Riley said.

"That's all for now," Meredith said. "Both of you go home and get some sleep."

*

When Riley parked at her home in Fredericksburg, she was struck by how quiet and still her neighborhood was. Just the night before last, the whole area had been flooded with cops and agents and medics. Now it looked quite peaceful, with discreet decorations adorning most of the front doors and artificial candles in some windows.

Riley wondered what the neighbors thought about the chaos and danger she had brought among them. Three people had been taken away in ambulances. The neighbors had ample cause for alarm.

Riley unlocked the front door and let herself into her townhouse. She more than half expected to hear someone call her name. She had seldom been in this house without the presence of April or Gabriela or both. Now her home was strangely devoid of life.

Yesterday she had put the broken chair and lamp out on the back deck to take care of later. The FBI had taken the fireplace poker that April used for a weapon. No doubt they would run routine DNA tests on the blood found on it, although it really was a

85

moot point. April's attacker had been Orin Rhodes. He'd been clearly identified from prison photographs.

When Riley sat down in the living room, it occurred to her that she hadn't communicated with April all day. There was no reason to worry about her, of course. She was in a safe place under close guard, and Riley would certainly have heard by now if she'd been in any danger. Even so, Riley felt an irrational pang of anxiety.

She flipped open her laptop computer, hoping it wasn't too late for a video chat. Riley dialed, and April quickly accepted the call. Riley could tell by her face that she wasn't in a good mood.

"Hi, Mom. What's going on?" April asked.

Riley saw no point in telling her all that had happened in Upstate New York. And she didn't want to alarm her any further about Orin Rhodes.

"I just thought I'd check in," Riley said. "I hope it's not too late."

"Naw, I couldn't sleep."

Riley could see that April was idly painting her fingernails.

"How are you doing?" Riley asked.

April sighed. "I'm bored. This place sucks."

"I know it's no resort," Riley said. "Just be patient. After this whole thing is over, we'll go somewhere nice."

April yawned. "No, after this is all over you'll be off on another case. Don't worry about it. I can handle it."

Her face perked up a little. "Oh, Dad came by today," she said.

Riley was a bit surprised. She wasn't aware that Ryan knew April's exact whereabouts. An agent had probably contacted him at April's request. Riley couldn't blame April and Ryan for wanting to see each other. But she hoped Ryan had handled his visit discreetly.

"How's he doing?" Riley asked.

"OK, I guess. He's still upset about what happened. And he agrees with me that this place sucks. He says I shouldn't be here. He says they should have put me someplace else."

Riley felt slightly rankled. It wasn't Ryan's decision to make, and she didn't like him putting ideas into April's head.

"You're staying right there where you're safe," Riley said.

"I know," April said.

She yawned again.

"I'm tired. Maybe I should go to sleep."

"You do that," Riley said. "I love you."

"I love you too."

They ended the chat. Riley got up from the couch and got a glass and a bottle of bourbon from a kitchen cabinet. She went back into the living room and poured herself a drink. She sipped it, and the warm sensation in her throat was welcome. She could feel her inner tension starting to unwind. This was just the thing she needed to relax.

Maybe I'll fall asleep right here, she thought.

She realized that one advantage to having the house all to herself was not having to worry about things like where she slept. Still, she was lonely, and looked forward to having both April and Gabriela home again.

*

Snow was swirling around Riley, so thick and blinding that she couldn't see where she was. She turned around and around, not knowing where to go or what to do.

Then she saw a shadowy figure some distance off. The person seemed to be running toward her. Maybe it was someone who was coming to help her. Or maybe it was someone who was coming to her for help. She had no idea.

As the figure came nearer, Riley could make out that it was a teenage girl. The swirling snow cleared a bit, and Riley saw that it was Heidi Wright. She was rushing headlong toward Riley, holding out a gun, aiming it directly at her.

Riley heard a voice call out sharply—

"Shoot her! What are you waiting for?"

—but she couldn't tell whose voice it was—her father's or Shane Hatcher's.

"I can't," Riley said. "It's just a kid."

"Do you want to live?" the voice demanded.

Then Riley heard a gunshot. It took her a moment to realize it was from her own Glock, the gun that she was holding in her hands. Everything changed. The swirling snow turned red, as if it were raining blood.

The girl tottered but didn't fall. Then she wasn't the girl anymore. She was Riley's mother, dead on her feet, her chest bleeding from the bullet wound that had killed her when Riley was just six years old, staring at Riley in mute horror.

"Mommy!" Riley cried out.

The high pitch of her voice surprised her. Then she realized that she was suddenly only six years old. She wanted to rush toward her mother, but her feet wouldn't move.

Then came that male voice again—and this time Riley could tell that it was her father, loud and clear.

87

"You're no good to anybody unless they're dead."

Riley's eyes snapped open, and she found herself lying on the couch in her living room. Morning sunlight was streaming in through the windows. The house was silent.

Riley groaned aloud as she remembered the dream. It had been a long time since she'd dreamed about her mother's death, and she'd spent her whole life trying to forget it. She had only been six when she'd seen her mother gunned down by a thug in a candy store. Even though Riley was just a little girl, her father never really forgave her for not stopping it from happening.

Whenever she had dreams like this, Riley wondered if she'd ever really forgiven herself.

She looked at the bottle and the glass on the coffee table. She remembered now that she'd only had a couple of drinks late last night before going to sleep. That was a good thing, considering how she sometimes drank more than she should in times of stress.

She walked to the kitchen and saw that no coffee was ready.

Of course not, she thought. *Gabriela's not here.*

She didn't like the thought of making and eating breakfast in her lonely home right now. She decided to take a shower, get dressed, and get coffee and breakfast at some fast food place.

She remembered Meredith telling her not to come around to the BAU right away. That was fine with her. There was someplace else she wanted to go.

*

When she got to the hospital, Riley was relieved to learn that Blaine was out of the ICU and in a private room. When she found him, he was awake and watching TV. His face was still bandaged on one side. He smiled when he saw her come through the door.

"Hey, I thought you were off catching bad guys," he said.

"I'll be doing that soon," Riley said, sitting beside his bed. "And I hope I can catch the bad guy who caused us all so much trouble."

"I'd really appreciate that," Blaine said.

They were both quiet for a moment. Riley felt a bit awkward. She wanted to hold his hand. But the hospital didn't feel like quite the right setting for such an intimate gesture, especially since neither one of them seemed to know exactly where their relationship was headed. She looked at him for a moment.

"How are you doing?" she asked.

"Pretty good," Blaine said. "A few aches and pains. They didn't find anything wrong with me except three broken ribs and a cracked face. I get to go home tomorrow. Crystal wants to come home, too. At least if you think it's safe."

Riley hesitated. She didn't want to make any false promises. Even so, she felt all but certain that Orin Rhodes had moved on to other prey.

"I think it's safe," she said.

"Good. Felicia's been taking good care of her."

Riley remembered the attractive woman who'd been at the hospital a couple of nights ago—Blaine's assistant manager at his restaurant, she'd said. Riley wondered if maybe she had a rival. But now was no time to worry about that.

"Blaine, I just want to know how grateful I am that you did what you did. You probably saved April's life. You could have just called 911, but help wouldn't have reached her in time. You were very brave."

"And stupid?" Blaine said with a smile.

Riley laughed a little. "Yes, and stupid. But stupid in the best possible way."

Blaine surprised her by suddenly taking her hand.

"There isn't much I wouldn't do for you and April," he said.

Riley didn't know what to say. She simply smiled and shared his quiet gaze. She was filled with a warm feeling toward this warm, kindly, attractive man. She more than half-wanted to crawl into the bed and cuddle up beside him.

She almost laughed at the idea of doing such a thing in a hospital. Now was definitely not the time or place.

But maybe under different circumstances, she thought.

Her phone buzzed. She saw that the call was from the BAU.

"I've got to take this," she told Blaine with a sigh.

Blaine let go of her hand and patted it gently. Riley got up and stepped out into the hallway.

When she took the call, she heard Walder's voice.

"Agent Paige, grab your bag and get over here," he said. "You're flying straight out to South Carolina."

"What's going on?" Riley asked.

"There's been a murder. Agents Huang and Creighton will brief you on the plane."

Without another word, Walder ended the call.

CHAPTER NINETEEN

When the little BAU jet took off, Riley still had no idea what this trip was all about.

"There's been a murder," Walder had told her over the phone. Riley knew nothing more than that.

She was sitting in the cabin next to Bill. Across a table facing them were Agents Emily Creighton and Craig Huang. Creighton and Huang were young and fairly inexperienced agents who nevertheless were Walder's favorites. Riley had always felt at odds with Creighton, who fancied herself a much better agent than she actually was. But Huang was starting to grow on Riley, and he was learning well.

Riley sensed from Creighton's smug expression that she and Huang and been fully briefed by Walder. No doubt Riley and Bill had deliberately been left out of the loop. It was just one of Walder's many little ways of expressing his dislike for Riley, and of making her feel unimportant.

It's almost working, Riley thought.

When the plane reached cruising altitude, Creighton opened up her laptop and set it on the table. She displayed a crime scene photograph of a murdered man lying face up in a wooded area. His clothing was dirty and bloodstained. He was fairly mangled by bullets—Riley guessed that that he'd been hit by nearly twenty rounds. One wound was squarely in the middle of his forehead. His eyes were wide open.

Riley shuddered as she realized that this victim been alive and fully conscious until the very last shot was fired.

"Kirby Steadman was a retired high school principal who lived in Worland, South Carolina," Creighton said. "He was killed yesterday morning at Elbow Lake State Park. A park ranger came across the body early in the afternoon."

Before Creighton could continue, Riley asked, "How far did he crawl from the shore of the lake?"

Creighton looked at Riley with surprise.

"How do you know he crawled from the lake shore?" she asked.

Riley pointed at the picture. "He's wearing a fishing vest," she said. "His pants are soiled at the knees. My guess is he was fishing when he was targeted and got hit with the first round. Then he tried to get away, and his attacker kept shooting him. How far did he get?"

Riley could tell by Creighton's displeased look that she'd guessed right. Huang smiled a little.

"He crawled about thirty feet," Creighton said.

"So what makes this a BAU case?" Bill asked.

"The local cops had no idea what to think of it at first," Huang explained. "Kirby Steadman had no enemies that anybody knew of. But then someone left a strange message on their call-in line."

Huang turned on a small recorder. Riley heard a familiar voice.

This is Shane the Chain. The body you just found at Elbow Lake isn't my handiwork. But Agent Riley Paige at Quantico will be interested. Let her know all about it.

Huang clicked off the recorder.

Creighton said to Riley, "I take it you can confirm whether or not that's Shane Hatcher's voice."

"It is," Riley said.

"And whose 'handiwork' do you think this murder is?" Creighton asked.

Riley remembered those random killings all those years ago in Jennings—the two victims who had been repeatedly, sadistically shot until they were executed.

"Orin Rhodes," Riley said.

Creighton nodded. "Agent Walder thinks so too. And based on the phone message, it seems that Shane Hatcher has also been in that area lately."

Then Creighton added with a malicious grin, "And you've got about three hours left to catch him."

Riley's face burned with anger. She knew that Creighton was simply repeating Walder's words. And of course, Walder knew perfectly well that Riley couldn't possibly meet his forty-eight-hour deadline. She'd be spending about half of the remaining time on the plane. Walder was just setting her up for a sharp reprimand. And he was planning to enjoy it.

Meanwhile, Creighton was obviously enjoying being in charge. She continued, "We'll be landing on an airstrip just outside of Worland. We'll go straight to the crime scene. After that, Agent Paige, you and Agent Jeffreys are under orders to hunt down and apprehend Hatcher."

Riley noticed that Bill was starting to look annoyed.

Bill said, "And what are you two going to do while Agent Paige and I are chasing down Hatcher?"

"We're going after Orin Rhodes," Creighton said.

Riley was seething now.

What does Walder think this is, a game?

She'd tried to tell Walder that Orin Rhodes was the real threat right now, not Hatcher. She and Bill ought to be working together with Creighton and Huang to bring him to justice before he killed again—and he certainly would kill again. They could go after Hatcher when that was done.

But Walder wasn't going to allow that. And he had no reason at all except to put Riley in her place. For the time being, he had succeeded.

Riley listened to the rest of Creighton's briefing in angry silence. The plane couldn't land soon enough to suit her.

*

About three hours later, Worland's police chief Lonny York was driving Riley, Bill, Huang, and Creighton through Elbow Lake State Park. Chief York was an enormous bear of a man approaching retirement age. Although the park's trees were barren this time of year, Riley could see that the forest must look glorious in spring and fall. She saw no snow anywhere.

As they approached their destination, Riley looked at her watch.

Time's up, she thought a bit wryly.

The deadline for catching Hatcher was passing at that very moment. Riley more than half expected her phone to ring, and for Walder to call and goad her about her failure. But no, she figured Walder would save his gloating for when she got back to Quantico.

As they neared the lake, Chief York pointed to one of the many cabins they had been passing.

"That's where the killer stayed," he said. "He'd been renting the place since Saturday morning."

As York parked the SUV in front of the cabin, Riley considered Rhodes' timeline. He must have driven here and rented this place shortly after he'd attacked April. He'd apparently spent a leisurely day here, and then killed Kirby Steadman the next morning, just yesterday. Now he was gone and he'd left no clues to his direction.

The five people got out of the SUV and headed straight toward the cabin, which was wrapped like a boxed gift in yellow police tape. They ducked under the tape and entered the cabin.

Riley looked around. With its smoky pine aroma, it reminded her of the cabin where her father had lived during his last years in the mountains of Virginia. The place didn't evoke pleasant memories, but she knew that it must seem charming to tourists who rented it.

Riley saw signs of fingerprint powder here and there.

"Did you find any prints?" she asked York.

"Yeah, lots of them," York said. "He made no effort to wipe the place down. Of course, he must have been in kind of a hurry to get out of here. It's been too soon for us to match the prints to anybody."

Riley had no doubt that at least some of the prints would belong to Orin Rhodes. But she wondered if Shane's prints might show up as well.

Riley, Bill, Huang, and Creighton looked around for a few moments. There wasn't much to see. Aside from fingerprints, the cabin's last occupant seemed to have left nothing behind.

She noticed several brochures lying on the dresser. They were the usual tourist stuff, advertising things visitors might like to see. But then she took a closer look. Three of them featured South Carolina tourist sites, two beach resorts and this very place, Elbow Lake State Park. The other two were about places in Florida, a historical and ecological preserve at Jacksonville and Everglades National Park down near Miami.

"Do the cabins always provide this kind of information for visitors?" she asked York.

"I don't know," the chief replied. "But they look pretty ordinary."

"They're probably not important," she said, but she tucked the brochures into her bag.

"Come on," York said. "I'll show you where Kirby was killed."

They all went outside, and Riley followed right behind Chief York as he led the way to the edge of the woods. In a moment, they were walking down a path that led to the lake.

Behind her, Riley heard Creighton say, "Too bad there's been no snow lately. We'd be able to trace his movements better."

But Riley knew that she'd have little trouble tracing Rhodes' movements. In fact, she was slipping into his frame of mind already. Of course, he'd walked along this very path on his way to kill his victim. But had he targeted Kirby Steadman already? Did he know that he'd find him here?

No. Riley sensed that he had no idea who he'd find at the lake, if he found anybody at all. And yet he was armed. Riley could imagine the weight of his semi-automatic pistol with its high-capacity magazine under his belt. It had been a good bit heavier than her Glock.

He'd been fully ready to kill if he encountered somebody—anybody. And he'd been prepared to do nothing at all if he encountered nobody.

Organized randomness, Riley thought.

That seemed to be crucial to his MO. He was fully prepared for whatever happened by chance.

Soon the path ended on the rocky shore of the lake. Riley's four companions stepped out onto the rocks, but Riley stopped in her tracks at the path's end. She pointed to a boulder on the water's edge.

"His fishing tackle was found over there, wasn't it?" she asked York.

"Yep," York said, sounding a little surprised.

But for Riley, it was an easy call. It was the ideal fishing spot—just exactly the spot her father would have chosen back when he took her fishing.

The impressions were becoming stronger now.

"Rhodes stands right here," Riley said, still standing at the end of the path. "He calls out to Kirby Steadman. Probably a friendly greeting. Kirby says something friendly in reply."

Riley pantomimed drawing the gun, aiming it, and firing it.

"Then he takes the first shot," she said.

She imagined the loud crack of the semi-automatic pistol across the lake. But no, that couldn't be right. All that noise would be too messy for him.

"He uses a silencer, so the shot isn't heard far away," she said. "He aims for somewhere on Steadman's extremities. He certainly doesn't want to kill him right away. He's more like a cat playing with a mouse."

Riley noticed that Creighton, Huang, and York were standing nearby watching and listening. She didn't much like that. True, she was well-known at the bureau for her ability to get inside a perpetrator's head. But it wasn't performance art. Bill had always understood that. These other three gawkers didn't.

"He doesn't fire his next shot right away," she said. "He waits for his prey to make a run for it."

Riley pointed along the line of trees.

"Steadman heads right over there, hoping to get away into the woods. Rhodes fires one shot before he gets there."

Riley pointed to a rock midway between the shore and the trees. Sure enough, there was a splash of dried blood there.

Riley followed Rhodes' footsteps toward the spot where Kirby had gone among the trees. No path was there, but a trail of broken-down underbrush marked where Kirby had crawled and flailed in a desperate quest for safety. Riley could see where blood had splashed on grass and leaves in several distinct places.

Still pointing her imaginary weapon at those spots, Riley continued along Rhodes' path.

"He follows right behind Kirby, firing here … and here … and here … some eighteen or nineteen rounds, and Kirby is still alive, pleading for mercy."

Finally she stood looking down at the spot where the weeds and brush were still crushed down in the shape of Kirby's body.

"He has one bullet left. He's determined to make it count."

She knelt down and pointed.

"So at point-blank range, he fires at Kirby's forehead. Kirby falls back dead. Rhodes goes back the way he came, and unhurriedly packs up his things and drives away."

Riley got to her feet and turned toward her four companions, who had been following her. Emily Creighton's arms were crossed and she had a slight smirk on her face. She was obviously trying her best to look thoroughly unimpressed.

"What about Hatcher?" Creighton asked.

"Pardon?" Riley said.

Creighton shrugged. "You're not here to catch Rhodes. You're here to catch Hatcher. And you've run out of time, haven't you? So what about him? Have you found out anything about him here?"

Riley didn't reply. She turned all around. No, Hatcher had left no physical traces that he'd been here. He was too deft, too cunning for that. But he *had* been here—perhaps minutes after Kirby had died. She couldn't prove it, but she felt it deep in her bones.

After all, it was just like Hatcher had told her:

"We're joined at the brain, Riley Paige."

CHAPTER TWENTY

A little while later, Riley glared at the unmarked loaner car that Huang and Creighton were driving away from the police station.

Do I really want to do this? she asked herself as she climbed behind the wheel of the similar vehicle that Chief York had provided for her and Bill. She started the engine.

"Oh, no, Riley," Bill said, watching her with a worried expression. "Don't even think about it."

"Think about what?" Riley asked.

"Following Huang and Creighton."

"Why not?"

Bill growled under his breath. "I can't even count the reasons. They're here to catch Rhodes. We're here to catch Hatcher. We're definitely *not* here to stalk our colleagues. What are you thinking, Riley?"

Riley didn't reply for a moment.

"Riley?" Bill said again.

"Look, Bill, we both know that trying to track down Hatcher right now is an exercise in futility."

"So you're going to try to track Rhodes instead?"

"I don't think that either of them is anywhere in the area now. We're all wasting our time here. I just want to know what Creighton is up to, even if I have to follow her all over South Carolina. And I'm going to be part of this whole investigation, whether she likes it or not."

Bill shook his head.

"You're going to get us both fired," he said.

Riley felt a pang of conscience. Bill was probably right. And it didn't seem fair. But her own course was set.

"Bill, if you don't want to go with me, that's all right. I'll drop you off right here, and you can head right back to the police station. Then you can do whatever you want to do."

"Never mind," Bill said with a note of resignation. "Let's do this your way."

Riley followed the car through Worland's little downtown area into a pleasant residential area. Creighton, who was driving, slowed the car down, apparently looking for an address. Riley started to get a hunch where she might be headed.

She's about to make a big mistake, Riley thought.

Maybe Riley could stop her from doing that. If not, maybe she could do some damage control.

Meanwhile, something was nagging Riley about the crime scene. Something didn't quite make sense. Not that she had any reason to expect Orin Rhodes' actions to make much sense. Still, there had been something wrong with how he'd left things.

Like he left something unfinished, she thought.

She couldn't put her finger on quite what it was.

Creighton parked in front of a charming old two-story house with stucco walls. Riley parked a couple of cars behind her.

"You can wait for me here if you want to, Bill," Riley said, giving him another out.

Bill shook his head.

"No, I've got a pretty good idea of what's going on. I'll go in with you."

When they both got out of the car, Emily Creighton was leaning against their car, waiting for them. She didn't look at all happy to see Riley. Craig Huang stood nearby, looking off in another direction as though he'd rather not be here at all.

"You didn't think you could tail me without my noticing, did you?" Creighton snapped.

"Naw, I just thought I'd come along and see if I could offer a helping hand," Riley replied with a smile.

Creighton crossed her arms and glared at Riley.

"You don't even know what Huang and I are here to do," she said.

"Oh, I think I do," Riley said. "And let me explain why it's a bad idea—"

"Save it, Agent Paige," Creighton said. "I know what I'm doing."

Huang glanced at Riley and shrugged uneasily, not looking nearly as confident as his partner. Nevertheless, he followed Creighton up the sidewalk toward the house. Riley followed right behind them, and so did Bill. Riley knew there really was no way for Creighton to stop them from joining her, not without making an embarrassing scene.

A worried-looking woman in her forties answered the door.

"Are you Ms. Steadman?" Creighton asked.

"Yes, I'm Cheryl Steadman," she said, looking a bit surprised.

"Is your husband home?"

"Yes."

Riley now knew that her hunch had been right. Creighton had come here to interview Kirby Steadman's nearest kin. As far as Riley was concerned, it was a perfectly terrible idea that couldn't yield any positive outcome. The local police had provided them with a transcript and recording of their own interview and Riley was sure that there was no connection between this unfortunate family and the murderer.

Creighton took out her badge, and so did Huang.

"I'm Agent Emily Creighton, FBI. This is my colleague, Agent Craig Huang."

She pointedly did not introduce Bill and Riley.

"May we come in and talk to you and your husband?" Creighton said.

"Is it really necessary?" Cheryl Steadman asked. "Gilbert is taking the news about his father awfully hard." She swallowed hard and added, "Now, of all times."

"We've just got a few questions," Creighton said.

Cheryl Steadman sighed and said, "We've answered so many already."

Then she warily opened the door and invited the four agents inside. She led them into the living room, where Gilbert Steadman was staring blankly into a fireplace. The flame had almost died away, but Steadman showed no interest in getting it going again.

Riley noted a little stray ribbon, a sparkle here and there. She realized that the Steadmans had hastily removed holiday decorations.

Like his wife, Steadman appeared to be in his late forties. Riley immediately noticed a striking family resemblance between him and the unlucky victim in the crime scene photos. Both men were tall, slim, and muscular.

"Gilbert, these people are from the FBI," Cheryl Steadman said. "They want to ask some questions."

With a gesture, she invited all four agents to sit down.

"We're sorry for your loss, Mr. Steadman," Creighton said.

Gilbert Steadman nodded.

"What have you found out?" he asked in a shaky voice. "The police haven't told us much."

"We're hoping you can help *us,* Mr. Steadman," Creighton said, trying to sound compassionate and concerned. Riley didn't find her at all convincing, and she was sure the Steadmans didn't either.

"I can't imagine how," Steadman said. "I've got nothing to tell you. Dad was a widower, a retired high school principal. He didn't have an enemy in the world. He liked to *fish,* for crying out loud. That's all he was trying to do when he—"

Steadman's voice choked before he could finish his sentence.

Creighton said, "Mr. Steadman, we believe your father was killed by a certain Orin Rhodes. Does that name mean anything to you?"

Steadman shook his head.

"How about you?" Creighton asked his wife.

"No," Cheryl Steadman said.

"Take some time to remember," Creighton said. "Orin Rhodes just finished serving a sixteen-year sentence in Sing Sing for killing six people. He came all the way to South Carolina to kill your father. There must have been some reason. Did your father ever spend any time in Upstate New York?"

Riley fidgeted, and Bill gave her a worried look. Things were going exactly as they'd both feared.

Steadman's eyes darted among the agents, trying to understand what was happening.

"No," he said. "He was born and raised right here, barely ever left the area. What are you getting at, anyway?"

Creighton's expression was harder now. Huang, who had said nothing so far, was starting to look uneasy.

"I need for you to think—both of you," Creighton said. "He must have said something—"

"He didn't," Steadman snapped, starting to sound angry.

Riley could see from Creighton's expression that she was gearing up to ask tougher questions. She couldn't let that happen.

Riley spoke in a firm tone, "Mr. and Mrs. Steadman, thank you for your time. We've got no more questions."

Creighton looked like she couldn't believe her ears. By contrast, Huang looked a bit relieved. Riley guessed that he'd had enough of his partner's arrogance for now.

Creighton started to protest. "Agent Paige—"

Huang interrupted her, "I think that we are actually through here."

Riley glowered at Creighton and repeated, "We've got no more questions."

Creighton ignored her partner, but she locked eyes with Riley.

Riley said firmly, "Agent Creighton, let's have a word outside."

Huang said a few parting words to the family and led the way outside. Riley and Bill followed him, and Creighton stormed out behind them.

As the four agents left the house and walked toward their vehicles, Creighton was completely irate.

"What the hell was that all about?" Creighton demanded.

"I'll tell you what it was all about," Riley snapped. "I just saved your ass big time. You were getting ready to badger a grieving son and his wife, for no reason at all."

"I knew what I was doing," Creighton said. "Either that man was having trouble remembering, or—"

"Or what?" Riley said. "He was lying?"

Creighton nodded slowly.

"Yeah, maybe he was. It makes sense, doesn't it? He's trying to protect his dad's memory. There's a family secret that he's wishing the whole world would forget. He's just got to know something. There had to be a reason for Orin Rhodes to come all the way down here and kill this particular man. There had to be a motive."

Riley could barely keep herself from shouting.

"There was no motive! It was completely meaningless! That's how Rhodes loves to operate. He prefers to kill randomly."

Creighton and Riley stood glaring at each other in silence for a moment. Bill and Huang looked extremely uncomfortable but both maintained their silence.

Trying to calm down, Riley said, "Agent Creighton, if I'd let you push any harder, it would have been a disaster. They'd have called in a complaint for sure."

Creighton's face was red and shaking with rage.

"Oh, there's going to be a complaint, all right," she said through clenched teeth.

Creighton got out her cell phone and started to dial. Riley knew perfectly well that she was calling Walder, to tell him that Riley had interfered with her investigation. And naturally, Walder was going to believe her.

Riley didn't feel like hanging around to listen. She started toward the car.

"There's going to be real trouble now," Bill said as he walked beside her.

"Don't I know it," Riley said. She knew that she'd hear about this soon.

CHAPTER TWENTY ONE

Riley dreaded what was coming next as she and Bill hurried toward the conference room early the next morning.

"Brace yourself," Riley told her partner. "This is going to be a rocky meeting."

"I know," Bill said with a sigh. "There sure haven't been any easy ones lately."

Shortly after Creighton had called in her complaint yesterday afternoon, Walder had ordered Riley and Bill to fly straight back to Quantico. Riley hadn't gotten much sleep last night. She was kept awake by the possibility that she would be out of a job tomorrow. When she had slept, she'd been bedeviled by familiar dreams. She still had wisps of memories of a flame in the darkness. She forced herself to concentrate, to clear her thoughts. She had no time now for old nightmares.

When they reached the conference room, Riley saw right away what she was in store for. Walder was sitting alone at the end of the long table. On the huge screen behind him was a daunting multimedia display. Technician Sam Flores was sitting to one side, controlling the images.

Meredith was conspicuously absent. Riley immediately guessed that Walder had pulled rank to make sure that Riley didn't have any allies present except for her partner. And Riley was feeling guiltier than even before that she'd gotten Bill mixed up in this fix she was in. But of course he had been there with her during the whole fiasco in South Carolina. And guilty or not, she was grateful that he was here now.

"Have a seat," Walder said.

Riley and Bill sat down without a word. Walder didn't speak for a few moments. He obviously wanted Riley to absorb at least some of the display.

It was a huge, constantly shifting collage of images, news stories, blog posts, and videos—all of them having to do with Hatcher's escape and the FBI's failure to catch him so far.

"Upstate New York Lives in Terror of Escaped Prisoner," read one headline.

"'Shane the Chain' at Large and Dangerous," read another.

"Local Police and Feds Helpless Against Murderous Escapee," read still another.

Several TV news videos were running, including one that showed law enforcement agents searching the countryside with bloodhounds.

There were sensational tabloid photos of Smokey Moran's body wrapped in chains. Other photos showed a burly-looking man Riley didn't recognize. One of the accompanying headlines read, *"Sing Sing Delivery Driver Missing and Presumed Dead."* It was, of course, the missing man who had been driving the truck in which Hatcher had escaped.

In the midst of all this, a digital clock display was dizzily running in microseconds ... *19:13.80 ... 81... 82 ... 83...*

Riley didn't need to be told that the clock was counting the time that had gone by since she'd missed her deadline to catch Hatcher. Walder wanted to rub in every passing second.

"We've obviously got a few things to discuss," Walder said in an ironic tone. "I've asked for Agent Creighton to join us."

For a moment, Riley wondered what he meant. Had Agent Creighton flown up to Quantico in the wee hours of the morning?

But no, Creighton's face suddenly appeared in the middle of the display. The meeting was, in fact, a video conference call.

Riley noticed that Craig Huang wasn't included in this call. Riley wasn't surprised. She remembered Huang's words of agreement when Riley called the misguided interview with the Steadmans to an end.

"We've got no more questions."

He'd been reasonable. He'd backed Riley up. So like Meredith, he was excluded from this meeting. Huang probably wasn't in anywhere near as much trouble as Riley, but he was definitely being kept on a tight leash.

Walder swiveled in his chair to face the screen.

"Agent Creighton," Walder said, "I'd like you to tell Paige and Jeffreys what you reported to me yesterday."

Creighton could hardly hide a smirk of smug satisfaction.

"Agent Paige and her partner muscled their way into an interview," she said. "Craig Huang and I were questioning Gilbert and Cheryl Steadman, the son and daughter-in-law of the murdered fisherman, in their home. The couple was hiding something, I'm sure of it. They knew something about Orin Rhodes. And if Agent Paige had let me ask just a few more questions—"

Bill interrupted in an angry voice.

"Now wait a minute. I was there. I saw what was going on. Agent Paige made the right call. The interview was going nowhere.

The Steadmans had never heard of Orin Rhodes until that very day."

Riley wanted to shush him. But she knew that it would do no good.

"Really?" Walder asked, leaning across the table toward Bill. "And just how did you know that?"

"I just know!" Bill said. "Agent Paige and I have got some three decades of experience between us. We know what we're doing. Our instincts are solid and our judgment is sound. Agents Huang and Creighton were just kids when we joined the Bureau. And frankly, Agent Creighton is acting like a kid right now—a rank amateur."

Creighton was finding it harder and harder to conceal her gloating.

She said, "Maybe you're right, Agent Jeffreys—about the Steadmans, I mean. But we'll never know now, will we? We tried to go back to pick up where we left off, but they won't talk to us now. What would have been the harm of letting me ask just a few questions?"

Bill snapped, "You were causing unnecessary distress to a grieving son and his wife. You were on the verge of treating them like criminals. And if Agent Paige hadn't put a stop to it, you'd have started accusing them of lying."

Walder glared across the table at both Riley and Bill.

"It was Creighton's call, not yours," he said. "You had no business being there at all." Turning to the screen, he added, "Agent Creighton, I want you and Huang to stay in South Carolina. See if you can get anybody else to talk. If the Steadmans are keeping any secrets, somebody in that town knows about it—friends, family, or neighbors."

"We'll get right on it," Creighton said.

"Thank you, Agent Creighton. That will be all for now."

"Yes, sir," Creighton said, beaming with pleasure as she disappeared from view.

Walder now turned his full indignation against Riley.

"Agent Paige, do I need to remind you of your deadline? You're now almost twenty hours behind schedule. I sent you to South Carolina to catch Shane Hatcher. You blew your opportunity. God only knows where he's gone by now. What were you thinking?"

Riley felt her face reddening with humiliation and anger.

She said, "I'm thinking that Orin Rhodes has tasted blood for the first time in sixteen years," she said, her voice shaking. "And he's remembering how much he likes it. He's just itching to do it again. And you've got two rookies chasing their own tails instead of stopping him. We all need to be together on this, sir. It's going to take our whole team to bring him in."

Walder shook his head.

"Agent Paige, if I didn't know better, I'd say you're in cahoots with Hatcher."

Riley's patience was gone. She was on the verge of letting forth a stream of profanities. Bill stopped her with a nudge of his elbow.

She took a deep breath and was silent for a moment. Then she took out her badge and gun and put them on the table.

"Here," she said to Walder. "I take it that these are what you're really after."

Walder looked like he was trying not to chuckle.

"Keep those, Agent Paige," he said. "You'll be needing them, at least for now. I'm giving you a chance to redeem yourself."

Redeem myself! Riley fought back another string of curses.

Walder continued, "You and Agent Jeffreys are going after Hatcher—in earnest this time. The first thing you've got to do is figure out where he is. Once you do, you'll go there and apprehend him, once and for all."

Then, after a pause, he said, "That will be all. I'll be expecting results by later today."

For a moment, Walder just stood there with a sneer on his freckled face.

Then he added, "Oh, and Happy New Year."

Riley and Bill got up and walked out of the conference room.

"Bill, I'm so sorry I got you mixed up in my problem," she said.

Bill laughed.

"Hey, don't mention it. One of these days, *I'll* be the loose cannon, and you can return the favor."

Riley laughed a little as well.

"Besides," Bill added, "you're right, and that baby-faced creep back there and his groveling protégé are wrong. We both know that."

Riley felt a lump of emotion in her throat as she walked at Bill's side. She had no words to express her gratitude for his constant loyalty.

"Have you had breakfast?" Bill asked. "Maybe we can go somewhere to eat, talk about our next move over some coffee."

Riley shook her head.

"I think I just need an hour or so to myself," she said. "I need to clear my head and think about where we go from here. I'll be in my office if you need me."

She and Bill parted, and she headed straight to her office. On her desk inside lay a flat FedEx envelope. The return address was in South Carolina. The name of the sender was "S. H. Friend."

Riley had to catch her breath. She knew in an instant that the package was from Shane Hatcher.

CHAPTER TWENTY TWO

Riley stood there staring down at the envelope, momentarily paralyzed with indecision. She was certain that it was from Shane Hatcher and that it might contain clues to his whereabouts. She thought that she should probably open it in the presence of another agent and list it as evidence. But she didn't want to wait. And she definitely didn't want to show the contents to Walder, at least not until she knew what those contents were.

She also knew that she was grappling with deeper issues than mere procedure. Opening this package alone and keeping it to herself might push her over a dangerous threshold that she didn't yet understand. But she simply couldn't imagine showing it to Walder right away. That might be the professional thing to do, but it wasn't an option.

Her hands trembling, she tore the envelope open.

Inside, she found three things—a sealed manila envelope, a white letter-sized envelope, and a large photograph. The photo was a picture of a smiling large-boned man sitting on a beach. Neatly written on the picture was a date—the day before yesterday—followed by a short message.

Wade Rosone sends his best regards from … ? As the song says, "You can't make old friends."

Riley recognized the face right away. She'd just seen this man's photograph in Walder's multimedia display. Wade Rosone was none other than the book truck driver who was missing and presumed dead.

So Hatcher hadn't killed him after all. The picture and the message gave Riley a pretty good idea of what had happened. Wade Rosone had been an "old friend," and a willing accomplice to Hatcher's escape. Hatcher had rewarded him with a pleasant retirement in some tropical paradise.

Riley had no idea where the money had come from. But Hatcher hadn't acted like someone short on funds. Now it seemed likely that he had somehow hoarded away an illicit fortune over the years. It occurred to her that he was probably a smart investor and that he would have ways of building up hidden bank accounts even from prison.

I'll never get to the bottom of all his secrets, Riley thought.

The question was, did she even want to?

Next she tore open the manila envelope. It contained a small handwritten note, pierced by a colorful fishing fly attached to a short length of fishing line. The note said:

Dedicated to Riley Paige ... I'm just getting started.

Riley could see at a glance that this handwriting was not Hatcher's. She wondered why that was. And what was the fishing fly supposed to mean?

Then something started to dawn on her. She remembered how lately she'd had a puzzling feeling that Rhodes had left the murder scene by the lake strangely incomplete.

Now she understood. Rhodes had actually left this note hooked by the fishing fly onto Kirby Steadman's body. But when Hatcher had arrived at the scene a short time later, he'd snatched the message away. And here at last were the note and the fishing fly— grim souvenirs sent to Riley by Hatcher himself.

But why? Riley wondered.

It didn't make sense. Hatcher had told her that he escaped solely to help her stop Rhodes. How had it been helpful to keep this note until just now? If anything, it seemed the opposite of helpful. It was as if Hatcher were toying with Riley, playing some kind of game with her.

She ripped open the smaller envelope. In it was a message in Hatcher's own handwriting.

Something is hidden in the room that never sees the sun.
Look inside the Cell.
And always ask yourself ...
"Am I already? Or am I becoming?"

She sighed with discouragement. Hatcher was communicating again in riddles. But the last words seemed especially personal, cryptic, and disturbing.

"Am I already? Or am I becoming?"

She had no idea how to answer.

CHAPTER TWENTY THREE

A little while later, Riley and Bill were on the FBI plane again, headed for Upstate New York. Riley alone understood the real reason why.

After reading Hatcher's message a few times, she thought she understood at least part of what he had meant. Surely the "room that never sees the sun" and "the Cell" referred to Rhodes' cell at Sing Sing. Hatcher seemed to be telling Riley that she'd find some vital clue there. So that was where Riley had to go.

Of course, she couldn't tell Walder anything about the package. And telling Bill would only put him at risk. So she'd convinced Walder that she and Bill needed to go back to Sing Sing in order to investigate Hatcher's escape. Walder had arranged for the use of the jet right away.

She was grateful that Bill wasn't asking her any questions.

Once the jet reached cruising level, Riley opened her laptop and dialed up April for a video chat. April answered, looking even more irritated than she had before.

"I just thought I'd check in on you," Riley said. "We haven't talked for a day or two."

April rolled her eyes. "Yeah, well, I guess you know it's New Year's Eve. Aren't you even coming by?"

"I'm sorry, sweetie, but I can't. I'm on a plane right now and I'll be out of the state."

"Yeah, well, this sucks more and more by the minute."

"Has your father come by again to see you?" Riley asked.

"Yeah. He comes every day."

Riley had mixed feelings about this. At long last, Ryan was showing true fatherly devotion. But was it really a good idea for him to show up at the safe house every day? What if someone was watching him? Riley wondered if maybe she should contact him and warn him about possible dangers. On the other hand, his visits were surely helping April to get through a bad situation.

"Daddy said he would come by sometime today," April continued. "But he has a party to go to later."

"April, I know this is unfair to you."

April blurted, "Mom, if I don't get out of here soon, I'm going to go batshit crazy. Don't get me wrong, Tara and Lucy are both great. But I'm so cooped up. I feel like I can't breathe."

"You've got to be patient for just a little while longer," Riley said.

"But how long is that?" April asked.

"As long as it takes," Riley said. She was startled by a note of impatience in her own voice.

April was quiet for a moment, then said, "So you're on a plane?"

"Yeah."

"On your way to catch a bad guy?"

"I'm on my way to Sing Sing prison looking for clues."

April's face had been growing more sullen by the second. Now she sounded angry.

"A prison, huh? Well, book me a room there, OK? It's got to be better than this place. I mean, as long as I'm never going home again—"

"April, that isn't fair. I'm doing everything I can—"

But April didn't give Riley a chance to say more.

"Goodbye, Mom," she said. Then she ended the call.

Riley sat there staring at the computer screen. She heard Bill's voice.

"Kid trouble?"

She looked over to where Bill was sitting. He'd been poring over his own laptop. Riley shook her head.

"I can't say I really blame her," she said. "She didn't ask for all this."

"It's not your fault," Bill said, with a warm smile of concern.

Riley didn't reply. She couldn't help but think that Bill was wrong. There had to have been something she could have done to keep April out of this terrible situation.

Even so, she smiled back at Bill. His sympathy meant the world to her—especially at a time like now. Again, she felt a flush of gratitude that he was in her life.

But she felt a pang of guilt as well. Although Bill hadn't said so, Riley felt sure that he knew that she wasn't telling him something. And yet here he was, at her side as always, not pressing her for details.

She felt a sudden unreasonable and impossible urge to change that.

"Bill, I want you to tell you—"

But Bill silenced her by raising his finger to his lips.

"Shh," he said. "No need."

Then he turned his attention back to his computer.

Riley felt strangely breathless, as if staggered under the weight of Bill's loyalty. As she sat there watching him work, she found herself remembering late last year, when April had fallen into the hands of Joel Lambert. Bill had been at her side then as well. And he'd done her a favor that had troubled her conscience ever since.

She remembered that fateful moment when she and Bill had found April, heavily drugged in a sordid room with Joel and a repulsive man who intended to have sex with her. Riley had implored Bill with a look to leave her alone with Joel.

With a simple nod, Bill had cuffed the would-be john and left the room. Riley had seized the opportunity to cause Joel gratuitous harm. The young man's hand would probably never heal properly.

No one knew what had happened except Joel himself, whose word meant nothing, and Bill. There would be hell to pay even now if anyone at the BAU ever found out about it. But she knew—absolutely knew—that she could trust Bill with the secret for the rest of their lives.

She briefly wondered, would she do the same for Bill in a similar situation?

It was a ridiculous question. She knew she would, without a second's pause.

But had it been the right thing for him to do? No—not if ethics and protocol had any meaning whatsoever. So had Riley's demand on Bill's loyalty forever tainted his integrity?

Loyalty takes some dark forms, she realized.

Loyalty also sometimes came at a terrible personal cost.

She turned away from Bill and closed her eyes. She found herself thinking again of Hatcher's cryptic riddle.

And always ask yourself ..."Am I already? Or am I becoming?"

She still didn't know what the words meant. But she didn't doubt that they were full of meaning. She also sensed that their meaning would become blazingly clear with some terrible self-revelation.

And then there was the song quote:

"You can't make old friends."

Was that how Hatcher was starting to see Riley—as an old friend, like Wade Rosone, bound by ties of savage, amoral loyalty?

And might he be right?

Riley tried to force such thoughts from her mind.

Get your head in the game, she told herself.

She and Bill would be at Sing Sing soon. Riley still had no idea what she might find there. She hoped that it would be something to lead her toward Orin Rhodes, the criminal she wasn't even supposed to be tracking.

CHAPTER TWENTY FOUR

Riley could tell that Guard Captain Garth Pyle didn't like her the moment she and Bill entered his office at Sing Sing. She didn't know why, but felt sure that she would soon find out. He was a powerful-looking man with a gravelly voice.

"Agent Riley Paige, huh?" Pyle grumbled after she and Bill introduced themselves. She detected a sneer in the curl of his lips.

"I take it you've heard of me," Riley said.

"Oh, yeah. You're Shane Hatcher's friend. Everybody here knows about your little visits. Tell me, what's Hatcher up to these days? Do you two stay in touch?"

Riley felt stung. The words were sarcastic, of course. Now she understood the feeling of hostility she was getting from him. The fact that she'd been in contact with a now-escaped prisoner didn't endear her to the prison staff.

She couldn't exactly blame Pyle for feeling this way. But his words cut closer to home than he could possibly realize. She couldn't exactly claim that she hadn't been in touch with Hatcher. He had forcefully communicated with her in Syracuse, but she couldn't begin to explain that to the captain. And she didn't want to mention that Hatcher had phoned her and then sent her materials that directed her here.

Riley said, "Actually, today I'm more interested in Orin Rhodes."

Pyle's eyebrows rose in surprise.

"The guy who was released about a week ago?" he said. "I can't imagine why. He was squeaky clean, a real goody two-shoes. The last I heard, he was headed back to his home town."

Riley was glad that the guard hadn't heard about the Rhodes case yet. It was bad enough that Hatcher was getting so much publicity.

"He didn't show up there," Bill said. "He just murdered a man down in South Carolina. Killed him slowly, filled him with nineteen bullets."

"Previous to that, he attacked my daughter in our own home," Riley added. "And he's not going to stop now. He's still at large."

Pyle looked truly taken aback.

"Well, I'll be," he said. "I hadn't heard about all that. I'd never have thought it."

"I'd like a look at his cell," Riley said.

Pyle shrugged.

"What would be the point?" he said. "He took all his belongings when he left. If he missed anything, the staff got rid of it by now. There's another prisoner there now."

Riley made no reply, and he finally said, "But if that's what you want, fine. Just don't expect a pleasant welcome."

Riley and Bill followed Pyle through a maze of gates and hallways. At last they came to the cellblock. It was lined on one side with high windows. On the other side was a staggering sight that took Riley's breath away—an entire cliff of cells, one row upon another rising up from the ground floor.

As they walked by them, Riley saw that the cells were tiny, with room for one prisoner each. Each cell had a bed, toilet, sink, and cabinet. Some had lots of belongings in them, while others were almost bare. Some prisoners had hung towels on the bars to give themselves a bit of privacy. Riley thought that the cells seemed like cages for animals.

As if to keep Riley from feeling any undue sympathy, the men in those cells were certainly acting like animals right then. At the sight of a woman, they unleashed a torrent of obscenities and catcalls, and groping arms reached out through the bars.

"Are you OK?" Bill asked with concern as Riley steered clear of the arms.

"Fine," Riley said.

"These guys are lucky not to have been here back when this place opened in 1828," Pyle said over the racket. "Total silence was imposed. If you made a peep, you could get a good beating with a cat o' nine tails."

The image jolted Riley with a disturbing memory. Just last year she'd hunted down a psychopath who had tormented women captives with a cat o' nine tails. She remembered her final confrontation with him in total darkness, and how he'd lashed her in the face with the whip. She still had a slight trace of a scar.

Snap out of it, she told herself. *You're here to do a job.*

A young guard came toward Riley, Bill, and Pyle.

"Well, here's a familiar face," he said, looking at Riley with an odd sort of smile.

"What are you talking about, Finney?" Pyle asked.

"Ask *her*," the guard said.

Riley had no idea what the guard meant.

The guard looked at her closely and said, "Weren't you Orin Rhodes' girlfriend or something?"

Riley was startled.

"What do you mean?" she asked.

"Well, Rhodes had plenty of pictures of you on the wall of his cell," the guard said. "Like an altar, almost. Right there among the Bibles and religious books and pictures of Jesus and such."

Now Riley felt slightly sickened. She knew that Rhodes' "altar" had been one of hatred and revenge. Was this why Hatcher had led her here—to find out just how deeply obsessed Rhodes had been with her? No, there had to be more to it than that.

Pyle told the guard, "This is FBI Agent Riley Paige."

The guard's expression suddenly seemed more respectful.

"Oh, Shane the Chain's pal. That's a whole different thing." Then he added with a grin, "Well, if you're here for a visit, I'm afraid you missed him. Didn't say when he might be coming back. Or maybe you happen to know."

A strange glint in the guard's eye disturbed Riley. Had this guard had something to do with Hatcher's escape? Surely he couldn't have managed it without help from inside. And judging from how richly the book truck driver had been rewarded, Hatcher clearly had a lot to offer a lowly prison guard.

And now what kind of connection did the guard imagine Riley had with Hatcher? A sour taste was rising in her mouth.

Pyle told the guard, "Paige is here to take a look at Rhodes' cell."

"It's just over here," the guard said.

He led Riley, Bill, and Pyle to a cell where a bearded giant of a prisoner lay on his bed. He had no belongings to speak of.

The guard said to the prisoner, "We've got a celebrity visitor, Hanford. This is none other than Agent Riley Paige of the FBI."

The prisoner sat up and looked at Riley with an expression of marked interest.

"Pleased to make your acquaintance," the prisoner said. "Shane the Chain said nothing but good things about you."

Ignoring the remark, Riley peered inside the cell.

The prisoner said, "Come on in for a look."

Riley glanced at Pyle, who looked back at her warily. She knew what he was thinking. Letting a reasonably attractive woman in one of these cells might be asking for trouble. Bill also looked distinctly uneasy.

But Riley wasn't frightened. And she figured she'd better make the most of the situation.

"Let me in," she told Pyle.

Pyle shrugged, then opened the barred door. He stepped back, fingering his baton and pepper spray canister.

The prisoner stood against the wall at the foot of the bed, leaving Riley free to look around. Riley kept her face angled toward him as she stooped down to look under the bed. He made no threatening moves.

Riley made a quick visual sweep of the room. There wasn't much to see. The cell had no nooks or crannies where anything might have been hidden away. Any evidence that Orin Rhodes might have kept here was surely long since gone.

She was learning something even so. The enormous prisoner was standing almost at attention, eyeing her with what seemed to be awed respect. Her connection to Hatcher carried tremendous importance here. Strange as it seemed, she was probably as safe in this cell with this convicted criminal as she was in her own home.

Probably safer, she thought, reminding herself of Rhodes' attack.

Again she remembered the song lyric Hatcher quoted in his message.

"You can't make old friends."

She shuddered to imagine what kinds of things Hatcher might have told the guard and the prisoner about their "friendship."

She stepped out of the cell, and Pyle shut the barred door behind her.

"Maybe you'd like a look at Hatcher's old cell while you're here," Pyle said.

Riley wondered whether it might be a good idea. She thought back to Hatcher's message.

Look inside the Cell.

He hadn't specifically said whose cell he meant. Was she looking in the wrong cell? In any case, what good would it do to check Hatcher's cell? By now, it would have been stripped of any possible evidence. Surely there was nothing left to see.

Then she remembered the other part of his message.

Something is hidden in the room that never sees the sun.

And at that moment, she felt the sun on her back. She turned around and stared at the high windows that faced the cliff of prison cells. She was a little angry with herself. She should have realized right away that Hatcher's description simply didn't fit this place. She had to come up with a new theory on the spot.

An idea started to occur to her.

She turned toward Finney, the guard.

"What do you remember about Rhodes' cell?" she asked. "You said he had pictures of me, Bibles, religious books, pictures of Jesus. What else did he have?"

"Nothing interesting," Finney said. "He studied a lot, so he always had quite a few books in there."

Riley's idea was coming into clearer focus. She said to Pyle, "I want to visit your library."

Pyle led them away from the cellblock through more gates and hallways until they got to the prison library. It was a large, single room with rows of bookshelves. Riley could immediately see that it had no windows at all.

"I think we're in the right place," she murmured to Bill.

But the right place for what? What was she supposed to look for here?

Then she remembered something else about Hatcher's note. What he'd written exactly was, "Look inside the *Cell.*"

The word "cell" was capitalized and underlined. Now Riley understood that Hatcher didn't mean any prison cell, and he didn't even mean the library. He meant something else.

"Give me a minute," Riley said to Bill.

She walked along the shelves looking at the subject descriptions. Soon she came to the section marked "SCIENCE."

She walked over to the section and browsed through the books. She quickly found a hefty textbook entitled *Cell Biology.*

Her breath quickened as she sensed that she was on the right track. She took the book off the shelf and thumbed through its pages. In the middle of the book she found a small clipping from a newspaper:

Furnished room.
Rent includes some furniture, electric, gas and water.
Cable/Telephone is extra.

The ad also included a phone number.

She hurried over to Bill with the piece of paper.

"I've got it, Bill," she said. "I know how to find him. We've just got to call this number."

Then Riley noticed that the librarian was staring at her. His face was lean and sinister, like a buzzard. And he was smiling at her. With a chill, Riley sensed that he knew exactly what she had found. He had known that the ad was there in the book. He had expected her to come looking for it.

How does he fit in? Riley wondered.

Her brain raced to put together a plausible scenario. Perhaps the librarian had noticed the ad when Orin Rhodes had returned the book. Then maybe he'd left the note in the book and notified Shane Hatcher about it, knowing that he'd be interested.

Riley strode up to the desk and glared at the librarian.

"What do you know?" she asked.

Still smiling, the librarian lightly shrugged.

"About what?" he asked.

"About *this*," Riley said, waving the scrap of paper in front of him.

The librarian seemed to be enjoying himself.

"Never seen it before in my life," he said.

Riley held his gaze. He didn't even blink and kept right on smiling. She knew there was no point in asking him further questions. He was doubtless part of Hatcher's network of "old friends." And how large and extensive was that network?

The driver had been part of it. Riley also suspected the guard named Finney, and the prisoner who now occupied Rhodes' cell. But she was sure that Hatcher had many more allies than that.

What chilled her to the bone was the thought that maybe she was becoming one of them herself. And maybe the librarian's smile was one of complicity.

Again she remembered what Hatcher had written:

And always ask yourself ...
"Am I already? Or am I becoming?"

Those questions were disturbing her more and more.

"Come on," she said to Bill. "Let's check this out."

CHAPTER TWENTY FIVE

Orin Rhodes was having a good time just sitting in a booth, eating a burger, swigging a beer, and wondering whether any of the people here would be his next victim. He enjoyed this noisy sports bar, with its loud music and various TVs blaring away. It was wonderfully different from the place where he'd been caged for so many years.

Tonight was New Year's Eve, and the customers looked like they were building up to a real party. He chuckled. He was likely to spoil the festivities for them.

Might his next victim be one of the guys playing pool? The garrulous bartender? The young woman at the jukebox? The depressed-looking man sitting at the bar getting drunk in the middle of the day? One of the two middle-aged women chattering at a nearby table?

Of course, he had no idea. And the fact that he had no idea made him smile. He'd kill, and he'd probably kill soon, but just *who* he was going to kill was out of his hands entirely. He was leaving it to chance.

He remembered his motto:

Chance is everything.

After all, he had chosen the fisherman in South Carolina by chance. And what a wonderful feeling it had been to kill him so slowly, knowing that the man himself had no idea why! It had been delicious—almost as delicious as the enormous hamburger he was eating right now.

Had he ever tasted a hamburger this good? If he had, it had been more than sixteen years ago, and he doubted that he'd had one this good even then. He wished Heidi could be here to taste a burger like this. Of course, everything he was doing was all for her. Even a tasty hamburger was somehow part of his revenge on her behalf. Freedom was sweeter than he'd imagined. But revenge was sweeter still.

Still, he knew he was going to have to curb his appetites. Since he'd been out, some skills from his youth had come back to him easily. He was still good at purse-snatching, picking pockets, and breaking into cars, and he had just stolen a sizeable tip that a party of six had left on a nearby table. He stole enough to get by, but he mustn't overspend. He'd put down a lot of money back in Virginia, paying a low-class private eye to follow a certain person. He hadn't quite built his stash back up where he liked to have it.

He finished the burger, left enough money to pay for it plus a tip, then went to the restroom. There he paused to look at his face in the mirror. Was it recognizable? The question mattered a lot right now. Since the South Carolina killing, his face had been in the news. But those pictures had been prison photos, and even though they'd been recent, he'd looked dour and unhappy in them.

Now he looked like a new man. After a week of freedom, his expression was relaxed and even happy. The cut on his left temple was healing well, and he was able to comb some hair over it. He'd also darkened his hair and let some stubble show on his chin.

He knew that he was really quite ordinary looking, except when he turned on his considerable charm. His looks served him well. He could blend in just about anywhere. Besides, he had put a lot of distance between himself and that lake in South Carolina. Nobody here was likely to suspect that he was in their midst, just waiting for blind chance to bring him new prey.

His face darkened a little when he thought about Riley Paige. How was she dealing with his escape? What was she doing right at that moment? Was she feeling appropriately pressured and guilty that he was killing innocent people because of her? Was she having any success at all at tracking him?

He'd left a few crumbs of information—or misinformation— here and there. He remembered the message he had left hooked to the fisherman's vest by the fishing fly.

Dedicated to Riley Paige ... I'm just getting started.

Had the message properly caught her attention? Now he worried a little. For all he really knew, the note hadn't gotten back to her at all. Was it possible that the redneck local cops had been too stupid to figure out who Riley Paige was?

And if the message had gotten to her, might she not have known who it was from? Might she have thought it was from a different murderer altogether? Maybe he should have signed his name to it. Or would that somehow have spoiled the effect?

Now was the time to decide. And it seemed wrong to sign the next message. He'd do just what he'd done before. He took out a pad of paper and jotted the message down, just to have it ready. This time he planned to attach it to the victim with a safety pin.

He left the restroom and went straight outside. The air was pleasantly warm, a refreshing change from the bitter cold farther north. And yet he paused just outside the door. There it was again— a strange feeling that he was being watched and followed. He'd been feeling it off and on for several days now.

Riley Paige, maybe? he wondered.

Surely she hadn't caught up with him, at least not yet. If she had, she'd have made her presence known by now. No, it wasn't her. Whenever she did find him, he'd know it, and he'd be ready for her.

He decided that the feeling was only his imagination. He put it out of his mind so that he could focus on whatever chance might bring next.

He walked out into the parking lot, admiring his own choice of the setting. He'd picked this place because it was isolated along a road near a small town. There were trees on both sides, and the road wasn't heavily traveled. Not a lot of people were here at midday, but he could still hear the noise of the televisions and music trailing behind him as he walked.

The sound faded as he walked across the parking lot toward his car. It was a large lot, with just a few cars clustered near the building. He had parked out on the far edge of the lot. A couple of other cars were over there too, probably belonging to employees.

Now that he was a safe distance away from the place, he took out his smartphone and set the countdown for ten minutes. The same as before, he would simply kill whoever happened along before ten minutes passed—if anybody did. He opened the door of his used car, took his pistol out of the glove compartment, and attached the suppressor to it. Then he put the weapon in his deep pocket and stood by his car and waited.

Before a whole minute had passed, the door to the bar opened and a woman came out. She was a short brunette, wearing a black skirt, a white shirt, and a black necktie—the uniform worn by the bar's employees. As she came nearer, he recognized her. She was the waitress who had served him his hamburger, and her nametag had said that her name was Amber. Apparently she had just gotten off work. And she was walking straight toward him.

Perfect, he thought.

She hurried across the lot toward an SUV that was parked near his. As she opened her car door, he headed casually toward her. He arrived at the car just as she was closing the door.

He smiled through the window and waved as if to ask a question. She smiled back and rolled down the window.

"Can I help you?" he said.

Now it was time to turn on the charm that had gotten him released from prison.

"Hey, you're Amber, right?"

"How did you know?" she asked.

"You waited on my table."

119

She nodded, pleased that he remembered her. "Oh, yeah," she said.

"I'm Tony," he said, pulling the name randomly out of his head.

"Pleased to meet you, Tony," she replied. She looked and sounded on the verge of being flirtatious. She had obviously taken an immediate liking to him.

He said, "I just drove in from New Orleans, and I'm going to be here for a couple of days. I was wondering if you might be able to suggest a good place to stay."

"Hmm, let me see ..."

As the woman knitted her brow in thought, Orin glanced toward the bar. The situation was perfect. There was no one in sight or within earshot, and if anyone did come out of the bar, he was shielded from view by the parked SUV.

He pulled out the pistol and stepped back just enough to put himself at point-blank range. He fired a shot square through the open window into the center of the woman's abdomen. The crack from the suppressor was even less audible than it had been at the lake.

The woman's body jumped exactly as if she'd gotten a sharp electric shock. Her eyes opened wide and stared at him. She opened her mouth but couldn't speak. Instead, she made strange gagging noises. Orin guessed that the bullet had hit her in the diaphragm, paralyzing her breathing.

Orin was fascinated. After the old fisherman's desperate pleading, this was going to be an entirely different kind of experience. But he was going to have to work fast in order to fire the eighteen remaining rounds while she remained conscious. He wanted her to be fully aware of every last bullet.

He opened the driver's door so that her whole body was a target. He fired shot after shot into her extremities, relishing the look of stunned and silent pain and horror on her face.

He wondered—would Riley Paige have a similar delicious expression when her own time came to die? Killing her would be the only death that he would deliberately plan. Once that was done, he'd be free to kill however he pleased—or however chance would have it.

He smiled that charming smile of his as he aimed the gun straight at the woman's forehead for the final and fatal shot. He hoped that somewhere, somehow, Heidi was watching and enjoying all this as much as he was.

CHAPTER TWENTY SIX

When the landlady let Bill and Riley into the small apartment, Riley was chilled by what she saw. A bed was unmade, an open soft drink can sat on a table with a half-full glass next to it, and some fast food wrappings were lying around. The place looked like somebody was living here right now.

Maybe Orin Rhodes just stepped out for a moment, she thought.

Could she and Bill be on the verge of catching him?

Riley walked over and looked at the liquid in the glass. A dead fly was floating there. No, the drink had been left here for several days.

Riley sighed. Catching Rhodes wasn't going to be as easy as she'd hoped.

The Philadelphia apartment had been easy to track down—perhaps too easy. Riley had called the number on the ad they'd found in the library book. The landlady, an elderly woman named Andrea Parisi, answered and confirmed that she recently had rented an apartment to a man named Orin Rhodes.

Bill had immediately called Quantico. He'd told Walder that they needed to fly to Philadelphia to check out a clue left by Shane Hatcher.

Well, it wasn't completely untrue, Riley thought as she remembered. At least, it was true that Hatcher had led them to the clue left in the Sing Sing library book.

She and Bill had come straight here on the FBI jet. They'd met Mrs. Parisi, shown her a photograph of Rhodes, and explained that he was a killer at large. She'd quickly agreed to let them search the apartment without a warrant.

"When did you last see him?" Riley asked as she searched between sofa cushions.

"Let's see," Mrs. Parisi said. "He took the room on Thursday. So I guess Friday morning was the last time. He didn't say where he went. I liked him so much, I hoped he'd come back."

The woman looked anxious and fretful.

"I had no idea there was anything wrong with him," she said. "He was so pleasant and polite. Are you sure you're looking for the right man?"

"We're sure," Bill said, looking inside a closet.

"Did he give you any kind of identification?" Riley asked.

"Yes, he showed me a driver's license. Now that I think of it, I'm afraid he fooled me about payment. When I asked for a deposit and proof of income, he promised to bring it in a couple of days. He said he had a brand new job and that he'd be getting paid soon. He paid in cash for a week, and I thought everything was all right."

Riley didn't say so, but she suspected that Mrs. Parisi was lucky to be alive.

Meanwhile, she wasn't finding anything of interest, and she could see that Bill wasn't either. Had this trip been a bust? Knowing that Orin Rhodes had been in Philadelphia last week told them absolutely nothing about where he might be now.

Then a possibility occurred to her.

"Could you check his mail?" she asked Mrs. Parisi.

"Certainly," she said. "I'll take you to the mailboxes."

Bill and Riley followed her down to the building's front entrance with its rows of metal mailboxes. Mrs. Parisi unlocked the one for Rhodes' apartment. Sure enough, there was an envelope inside. Mrs. Parisi handed it to Riley.

It was addressed to Orin Rhodes, printed neatly by hand. There was no return address. But Riley noticed that it was postmarked from Ossining, New York, on Tuesday of last week.

Riley opened the envelope and found a single sheet of paper inside. Also hand-printed was a short message.

Glad you like the house in the picture. It will suit your purposes well. You'll be expected there very soon.

The note was unsigned. Even though the printing was deliberate and meticulous, Riley wondered if perhaps it could be analyzed. But she doubted very much that the writer had left any fingerprints.

Bill stood next to her looking at the note.

"Sounds like someone arranged for a hideout for Rhodes," he said.

Riley nodded in agreement. "Did you find a picture of a house when you searched the place?" she asked Bill.

"I didn't find any pictures at all," Bill said.

"Neither did I. He must have taken it with him. Or thrown it away."

Riley stood puzzling over the letter for a moment. It seemed that Orin Rhodes had left the apartment before the letter had arrived. Did that mean that Orin Rhodes hadn't gone to the house in question? And even if he had, where on earth might it be?

"It looks like he's got an accomplice," Bill said.

Riley silently agreed. The possibility worried her more than she wanted to say.

At that moment, Bill's phone rang. He answered it, then said to Riley, "It's Walder. He wants to talk to both of us."

Bill put his phone on speaker. Walder sounded even more irritable than usual.

"There's been another murder," Walder said. "Down in Florida, in a little town near Jacksonville called Apex. A woman this time, shot nineteen times like Kirby Steadman."

Bill gave Riley a questioning look. Riley knew what he was thinking. Why was Walder calling them about another Rhodes killing? As far as Walder was concerned, they were tracking down Hatcher and only Hatcher.

"The body was found pretty quickly in a parking lot," Walder said. "But before the police could even get to the scene, they got another phone tip. From Shane Hatcher."

Riley and Bill stood staring at each other in silence.

Walder sounded angrier. "Paige, Jeffreys, I think we're getting played. Hatcher and Rhodes are in on this together. They're killing as a team—both the murder in South Carolina, and now this."

Riley didn't reply. She couldn't prove otherwise, and she wasn't going to argue with him over the phone.

"You two should have figured this out," Walder said. "You should have caught Hatcher by now. And so we've got another death. What the hell are you doing in Philadelphia? Get on the damn plane and fly straight down to Jacksonville. I'll have agents from the local field office meet you at the airport. And I'm sending Creighton and Huang to keep you two from screwing things up more than you already have."

Without waiting for a reply, Walder ended the call.

"Congratulations," Bill said. "You're back on the Rhodes case."

Riley understood the note of irony in Bill's voice. As far as she was concerned, she'd never been off the Rhodes case.

At least Walder's sending me where I want to go, she thought.

*

It was late afternoon by the time Riley and Bill were back on the jet flying down to Jacksonville. Sitting beside Bill, Riley stared out the window at the landscape below.

"What's on your mind?" Bill asked.

Riley just shook her head. She didn't want to drag Bill into the morass of trouble she was getting herself into. Apparently sensing this, Bill patted her gently on the hand.

"Look, I know you're doing some things that aren't by the book," he said. "I get that. And I know you're trying to protect me. But I think it's time to stop. We're never at our best together when we're keeping secrets."

Riley felt a lump in her throat. Bill was not only her partner but also her best friend. Not telling him the whole truth didn't seem right.

Bill added, "If you're going rogue, I'll just have to go rogue with you. That's the way it is. We're partners."

Riley's eyes stung a little. At last she knew that Bill's loyalty toward her trumped even his loyalty to the FBI. And for the first time, she realized that she felt the same way about him. The time really had come for her to tell him the truth.

"I've been in closer communication with Hatcher than I've been letting on," she said. "And my relationship with him is getting kind of … well, complicated."

Bill nodded. "Tell me," he said.

"When I encountered him back in Syracuse, he told me more than I told anybody else—including you. I know this sounds crazy, but he seemed to be genuinely concerned about me. He told me about Rhodes, and how he was out for revenge against me. And he was right. The attack on April proved it."

Riley paused for a moment.

"He said he felt some kind of special connection with me," she said. "He told me we're 'joined at the brain.'"

"Jesus," Bill said.

"But there's more. I got a package from him in Quantico, just before you and I went to Sing Sing. He wanted me to know he didn't kill the driver of the book truck. He rewarded him with a handsome retirement somewhere."

Bill looked a bit skeptical.

"Do you really believe that?"

"I think so. It's consistent with what I know about him. And he gave me the clues that helped me find that ad in the library book."

Riley felt relieved to be able to talk things out like this. It helped her to sort out her own confusion.

"But he's doing some things I don't understand. It turns out that Rhodes left a note on Kirby Steadman's body. Rhodes wrote, 'Dedicated to Riley Paige … I'm just getting started.'"

"Why didn't the local cops find the note?" Bill asked.

"Because Hatcher took it. He picked it up off the body before the police got there. And he sent the note to me in the package. I don't know why. If he's trying to help me, why is he teasing me like that? Why is he playing games? Why is he communicating in riddles? He acts like he wants me to learn something about myself. I have no idea what."

Riley sat staring out the window for a moment.

"And now I've got something new worrying me," she said. "That note somebody mailed to Rhodes—the note about the house. Who sent it? Might it have been Hatcher? Maybe I've got this all wrong, Bill. Maybe Walder's right. Maybe Hatcher's been in cahoots with Rhodes all along. Maybe Rhodes even helped him escape. And if that's true …"

She couldn't bring herself to finish the thought. What worried her now was that both Hatcher and Rhodes were manipulating her. Maybe she was nothing but Hatcher's dupe. If that was true, she'd completely lost her way as an agent. Perhaps she'd even lost her way as a human being.

Bill patted her hand again.

"We'll work this out," he said. "We're in this together."

Riley wanted to take comfort in Bill's words. But worries were gnawing away at her. Who was she really hunting—Hatcher, Rhodes, or both?

Or maybe I'm the only one being hunted, she thought with dread.

CHAPTER TWENTY SEVEN

When April's father showed up at the motel, April quickly shut the door that separated her from Darlene Olsen, the agent who was on duty that night. Breathless with excitement, she spoke to her father in a low voice so Darlene couldn't hear.

"Daddy, you've got to get me out of here," she said.

Her father's eyes widened.

"What do you mean?" he asked.

"What do you *think* I mean? This place is the pits. Everything about it sucks. Even the food sucks. You said so yourself, remember? It's not so bad when Lucy is here. I know her and she's fun to talk to. Tara's OK too. But Darlene is a bore. She doesn't do anything except sit over in the other room and watch stuff on her computer."

April's father looked all around the room with a look of distaste.

"I know how you feel," he said. "I can't imagine why they picked this place. Surely they have some better accommodations for people who need protecting. But this is all about keeping you safe."

"I don't see why staying safe has to be so boring."

Her father didn't look at all convinced. He just sat down and commented, "April, it is what it is. There's a good reason for keeping you well guarded."

"I've been here five days. Nobody has tried to hurt me."

"That just proves the point," he replied. "It is safe here."

April rolled her eyes.

"Oh, for crying out loud," she said. "I could be safe anywhere if you're around. I mean, you own a gun, right? You could protect me if you had to."

"That's not really the point."

"Then what is?"

Her dad didn't answer. April decided to play to his sense of guilt.

"I haven't had much of a holiday, being cooped up here. I'm sure I've missed some parties with my friends from school."

"There will be other holidays," he said. "And you and I have had some nice visits."

"But you've only got time to come by and see me for maybe a half hour every day. Sure, it's the same old story—the story of my life."

Her father looked hurt now. Her tactic was working.

"That's not fair," he said. "I know I've been like that in the past, but I'm trying to change. If I thought it would do any good, I'd cancel everything I've got going on. I'd do it right now."

"Well, why don't you?"

April's father paced the room uneasily as April sat on the bed.

"These FBI people are professionals," he said. "They do know what they're doing. Where do you think you and I could go where you'd be safe? You weren't safe at your mother's house, that's for sure. And this guy who attacked you surely knows where I live."

"But you've got a gun!" April said. "Are you scared or something?"

"You bet I'm scared. You should be scared too. We'd both be crazy not to be scared. Even the FBI doesn't know where the man who attacked you is right now. He could be looking for you at this very minute. Where do you think he'd look next?"

Her father sat down on the bed next to her. They both said nothing for a moment.

"Hey, I've got an idea," she finally said. "Let's go take a vacation together. We can go tonight. We can start the New Year off better than this."

April's father shook his head.

"It wouldn't be safe for you to go out in public," he said.

"It's night, Daddy. No one would see us go. And how would the bad guy ever guess where we'd gone? Even *we* don't know where we're going yet!"

Her dad smiled a little. April could feel that she was weakening his resolve. She knew that she could never manipulate her mother like this. Her father was an easier sell.

"Daddy, when I was little, you and Mom took me to Chincoteague to see the pony roundup."

Her father's smile widened.

"I remember. You wanted us to buy one for you. But we didn't have a place to keep a pony."

"They were so adorable."

April paused a moment, then added, "We could go back there right now. We could drive there tonight."

Her father's brow knitted with thought. April could see that he was seriously thinking it over.

"But it's winter," he said. "There's no pony roundup in February."

"But that means the whole place will be pretty much deserted. No one would look for me there right now. And the scenery will be nice. We could be on the water. And don't worry, I wouldn't ask for a pony this time."

They both chuckled a bit.

"Let's check out some places," her father said.

They opened April's laptop, and April's father started to shop for places to stay.

"Here are some motels," he said, pointing to a list.

April sighed loudly.

"Oh, Daddy, puh-lease! Not another motel!"

She took over the laptop and ran a search of her own. She quickly found a listing for a tall house with lots of balconies and porches looking out over the water.

"Here's what we need," she said. "A nice house for rent, right by the water. There's a garage at ground level, so we can pull right into it and no one will know who is staying there. It'll be nice, and I bet it'll be safer than a motel. Nobody will even see us go in there."

"You won't be able to go outside," her father said.

"Yeah, I get that. It's OK. This place has lots of room and a great view. You can go out and do whatever shopping we need, or we can get stuff delivered."

April's father sat staring at the ad for the house. Then with a smile, he quickly started making the reservation. April ran around the room grabbing her belongings.

"Are you really skipping your party?" April asked.

"Yes, I am," her dad said proudly. "I'll let them know later."

He quickly finished up on the computer.

"OK, that does it," he said. "Let's go."

"Wait a minute!" April said. "We can't just walk out of here. A couple of agents are sitting in a car outside. We've got to tell Darlene."

April hurried over to the door between the rooms and opened it. She waved for her father to come over. He didn't look very confident. April understood why. They were probably about to break a dozen or so rules. She hoped that the two of them could pull it off.

"My daughter and I are leaving," April's father told Darlene.

Darlene looked completely taken aback.

"Where are you going?" she asked.

"I'm taking April someplace else," he said, his voice sounding surer. "This place is completely unsuitable. And frankly, I don't think you're keeping her very safe here. I can do much better."

Darlene seemed to be very confused now.

"Sir, I'm not sure this is your decision to make," she said.

"It is my decision, and it's my right," April's father said. "She's a minor, and I'm her legal parent and guardian. You've been keeping her here with my tacit permission. Now I've changed my mind."

Darlene looked dumbly back and forth between April and her father.

April's father added, "I'm a lawyer. I know what I'm talking about."

April could see that Darlene was wavering.

"I should call her mother and let her know," Darlene said.

Without stopping to think, April blurted, "We called her already. She agrees with Daddy. She's fine with us getting out of here."

April didn't dare look at her father. She knew that he was surely horrified by her brazen lie. But at least he didn't contradict her.

"All right then," Darlene said. "I'll let the agents outside know."

She got on her radio and called the agents sitting in the car. April grabbed her bag and ushered her father to the front door, anxious to get out before somebody changed their mind.

As they walked out into the parking lot, April could see the FBI car parked inconspicuously nearby. She couldn't see the people inside very well, but at least they weren't jumping out of the car to stop her.

"You shouldn't have lied about your mother," April's father said as they headed toward his car.

April giggled. "What about you? 'I'm a lawyer. I know what I'm talking about.' Did you really have any idea whether you had any right to get me out of there?"

Her father let out a reluctant-sounding chuckle.

"No, I wasn't sure, I guess," he said. "I'm a business lawyer."

"OK, then. Let's get out of here. We can let Mom know after we get there."

April felt positively giddy as she climbed into the passenger side of her father's car. Just knowing that she and Daddy had bluffed their way out of an FBI safe house made this whole thing even cooler.

CHAPTER TWENTY EIGHT

Riley leaned forward to get a closer look at Amber Turner's bullet-riddled body. It was night, and she was using her flashlight because the parking lot wasn't illuminated well enough for examining details. The dead young woman's wide-open eyes seemed to stare straight at Riley, as if to ask her:

Why?

Riley wished she had an answer. But there never really was an adequate explanation for crimes like these. She felt a familiar bitterness in the pit of her stomach.

Bill stood at her side, adding the beam of his flashlight to her own.

"Happened in broad daylight," he said. "It must have been quite a shock to the guy who found her."

A restaurant customer had found the body that afternoon. It was splayed in the driver's seat of an SUV in a parking lot a short distance away from the sports bar. Riley's flashlight beam fell on a note fastened to the woman's jacket. She'd been told about that, and she bent closer to read it.

To Riley Paige ... Are you paying attention?

It was written on the same kind of paper as the note Hatcher had sent her—the note he had snatched from the fisherman's body. For some reason, Hatcher hadn't taken the note this time. Even so, Riley was sure that he'd been here. He'd reported the crime to the local police, after all.

Riley gingerly removed the note from the body and handed it to Bill.

"Let's bag this as evidence," she said.

As she continued examining the body, Riley wondered whether Walder was right after all. Were Hatcher and Rhodes working as a team?

Riley took a deep breath and tried to imagine the murder as it had unfolded. Might Hatcher have been the actual triggerman? She simply couldn't believe it. He'd never used a gun in a crime, and she was sure he hadn't started now.

No, Rhodes himself had fired the shots, Riley was sure of that. But had Hatcher participated in some way? Was he the seasoned veteran somehow guiding or mentoring the younger Rhodes? Might he have even stood at Rhodes' side while he committed the murder?

It didn't feel right to her. The more she thought about it, the more she felt sure that Walder was wrong. Hatcher would never team up with a guy like Rhodes—or with anybody else. It just wasn't in his nature. He was too solitary. And besides all that, she felt sure that Hatcher would consider Rhodes beneath him.

Nevertheless, the call left no question that Hatcher had been here.

Riley glanced at the woods along the edges of the parking lot. She knew that the area had been searched already. But Hatcher was nothing if not elusive. Perhaps he was out there watching right now.

If so, what was he doing here, trailing Rhodes' every step? And if he wasn't joining up with the random killer, then why was he tracking him? Or what was Shane Hatcher hunting?

Peering at the wounds, Bill said, "Looks a lot like Kirby Steadman's body at the lake."

"There are some differences," Riley said. "The killer wanted Steadman to crawl and plead. He didn't want that this time. It was broad daylight in a public place. He needed for the victim to stay put."

Riley pointed to a wound in the center of the woman's abdomen.

"That was his first round," she said. "It immobilized her but didn't kill her, didn't render her unconscious. But even though these shots were fired at point-blank range, they're a little sloppier than the killing at the lake. He was in more of a hurry, partly because he wanted the victim to be alive the whole time, partly because he was out in the open and might be seen. The suppressor on his gun kept the noise down."

Bill added, "The noise from the bar would have covered the slight sound his pistol did make."

Riley pointed to the wound in the forehead.

"The last round hit there."

A local cop walked toward Riley and Bill.

"That guy over there wants to talk to you," he said.

He pointed to a young man sitting on a low wall just beyond the yellow crime scene tape.

Riley and Bill walked over to him. Riley thought she detected a family resemblance to the unfortunate woman in the SUV—the same dark curly hair, the same roundish facial shape. He looked deeply stunned.

"I'm Riley Paige, FBI," she said, showing him her badge. "This is my partner, Bill Jeffreys. What's your name, sir?"

"Roy Turner," he said in a low, mechanical voice. "I'm ... I was ... Amber's brother."

"Did you witness the murder?" Bill asked.

The man shook his head.

"I got a call soon after ... it happened. I came over. I've been sitting here since I got here."

He fell silent for a moment.

"We're sorry for your loss," Bill said.

The man nodded silently again.

"You wanted to talk to us?" Riley said.

"Well, yeah," the man said. "What do you know? Who did this? Why?"

Riley fought down a discouraged sigh. There it was again, that question:

Why?

She crouched down in front of him and spoke in a soothing tone.

"Mr. Turner, I'm sorry to say this, but we don't know anything for certain yet. You must try to be patient."

He looked at her with a pleading expression.

"But surely you've got some idea," he said. "This is just a little town. How long is it going to take?"

Riley's heart went out to the young man. But she knew she had to weigh her words carefully. As much as she wanted to promise him that there would be answers soon, she simply couldn't do that.

She was grateful when Bill spoke up.

"Do the police have your contact information?" he asked.

The man nodded.

"Then I think you should go home," Bill said. "You should try to get some rest. You'll be contacted as soon as we know anything."

Without another word, the man numbly got to his feet and walked away.

Riley heard the crackle of a police radio. A local cop came over to her and Bill.

"You're wanted in the bar," he said.

Riley nodded. As she and Bill headed toward the bar, Riley looked over at the medical examiner. He and his team were standing next to their van, waiting patiently. Riley nodded as a signal that they could take the body away and the team strode efficiently toward the SUV.

Riley and Bill went inside the bar. Emily Creighton and Craig Huang had gotten here earlier. They had turned the bar into an improvised command center for local cops and a couple of FBI agents from the Jacksonville field office.

A handful of customers and employees had been kept here for further questioning. Riley and Bill walked over to Creighton and Huang, who were sitting at a computer.

"We're looking at the bar's surveillance video," Creighton said.

"Any luck?" Bill asked.

"The quality is lousy," Huang said.

Riley looked at the screen and saw that Huang was right. Whoever had installed the camera outside obviously hadn't expected it to be used for such a dire purpose. The image was grainy, and the angle gave a better view of the tops of people's heads than of their faces. Many of the people in those images, especially the men, looked exactly alike. The video wasn't likely to be very helpful.

Riley looked around the bar at the people who had been waiting. She picked out a person to talk to—a beefy guy on the edge of being overweight. She could tell by his face that he was normally happy and outgoing. Now he looked terribly distraught. The expression seemed rather incongruous on that particular face.

Riley introduced herself and Bill.

"I'm Marty Hollister," the man said. "I was bartending when I saw all the cops outside. I didn't know what had happened until I came out and saw—"

He couldn't finish the sentence. Riley sensed the reason for his anguish.

"She was your girlfriend, wasn't she?" Riley said.

Marty Hollister nodded.

"We're very sorry," Bill said.

Riley took out her cell phone and brought up a photo of Shane Hatcher.

She said, "Could you tell me if you saw this man today? Either in the bar or elsewhere?"

Hollister shook his head as he looked at the large, dark, and imposing man in the picture.

"I think I'd notice that guy," he said. "We don't get a lot of strangers in here. Apex isn't any kind of tourist town. There's nothing for people to see or do."

Then Riley brought up a prison photo of Orin Rhodes.

"What about this man?" Riley asked.

Hollister squinted at the photo.

"I don't know," he said. "I saw her waiting on a guy before she left. I didn't recognize him, so I don't guess he was from around here. He looked pretty ordinary, and I didn't really pay much attention. He could have been this guy, I guess. But his hair was darker. And he had some stubble on his face."

Riley felt encouraged. But before she could ask any more questions, she heard Creighton call out.

"Jeffreys, Paige—get over here. Walder's on video chat."

Riley and Bill sat down at the table with Creighton and Huang. Walder's disagreeable face glared from Creighton's laptop.

"What have you got?" Walder asked the team tersely. "It had better be good. We're under huge pressure to bring in Hatcher."

Riley stifled a groan. Walder's fixation on Hatcher instead of Rhodes was really annoying her.

"I was just talking to the bartender," Riley said. "He might have seen Rhodes. He thinks Rhodes might have been the woman's last customer before she went out to her car and got killed."

"'Might have been'?" Walder asked.

Riley bristled at his scornful tone.

"Yeah, might have been," Riley said. "A positive identification is going to be hard to come by. The surveillance footage is especially lousy."

"How about Hatcher?" Walder asked. "Did anybody see him?"

"The bartender didn't think so," Riley said. "And I don't think he would have missed him."

Walder sat glowering for a moment.

"Has anybody interviewed anybody in the victim's family?" he asked.

Bill said, "Agent Paige and I just had a few words with her brother out in the parking lot?"

"'A few words'?" Walder grumbled. "Doesn't sound like much of an interview. Does he have any idea what connection she may have had to Hatcher or Rhodes—or both?"

Riley and Bill looked at each other. Of course it hadn't occurred to them to ask. The idea was simply too far-fetched.

Riley said, "I'm sure the woman didn't have any connection to either of them, sir."

"You're 'sure'?" Walder echoed, sounding more and more incredulous. "Did you happen to ask him?"

"We did not, sir," Riley said.

"What about the bartender? Did you ask him?"

"No, sir," Riley said.

She didn't know who was getting angrier—Walder or herself. The team chief's sheer denseness about the matter exasperated her.

"Well, you'd better get back to it," Walder said. "Go talk to both of them right now—and every other friend or relative the woman had."

Riley had finally had enough.

"It's a waste of time, sir," she blurted. "These killings are random, meaningless. It's just like back in South Carolina. Did Huang and Creighton ever interview anybody who suggested that Kirby Steadman had any connection to either Hatcher or Rhodes?"

This time it was Creighton's turn to grumble.

"We didn't—no thanks to you," she said.

Riley knew that Creighton was still holding a grudge about how Riley had cut short that interview with Kirby Steadman's son and daughter-in-law.

"There *are* no connections," Riley insisted. "I know it sounds crazy that Rhodes has come all the way down to South Carolina and now Florida looking for random victims, but that's exactly what he's doing. I don't know why, but I'm sure it's true. And Hatcher's not helping him. Meaningless murders just aren't his style."

Walder continued to glare at Riley in silence for a moment.

Finally he said, "You haven't filed a report on what happened in Philadelphia. Did you find anything there?"

Riley said, "We went to a room that Rhodes had rented, and—"

The words were out before she'd had time to think.

"A room that *Rhodes* had rented?" Walder snapped.

"Yes, sir," Riley said.

She knew she'd stumbled badly. Now she braced herself for the worst.

"Agent Paige," Walder said in a slow, severe voice, "when you requested the use of the jet to fly to Philadelphia, you said you were checking out a clue left by Hatcher."

"And I was, sir," Riley said. "It was a note left in a book in the—"

Walder interrupted.

"And now you're telling me you went to check out a room Rhodes rented."

"Yes, sir," Riley said. "We didn't find anything except—"

But before she could tell him about the cryptic note in the mail, Walder interrupted again.

"Agent Paige, that's enough. You're off the case."

Riley gulped.

"Which case, sir?"

"Rhodes, Hatcher—they're really the same case now, so it doesn't matter. And I mean immediately."

Riley could tell that Bill had been doing his best to be quiet. But he couldn't do it anymore.

"Sir, what about me? I went with her, I was in the loop, I knew what she was doing."

It wasn't exactly the truth, and Riley knew it. She'd only filled Bill in on her involvement with Hatcher during the flight down from Philadelphia. As much as she appreciated his loyalty, she wished he'd keep his mouth shut, for his own sake.

Bill said, "You can't take her off the case and not me too."

"I most certainly can, Agent Jeffreys," Walder said. "We'll deal with your insubordination later on. Right now I need to you to keep working with Huang and Creighton."

Riley sensed that Bill was about to protest. She gave him a sharp nudge to silence him. Then she got up from her chair and headed for the door. In a flash, Bill was on his feet and walking beside her.

"I'm not putting up with this, Riley," he said. "If you go, I go."

Riley stopped in her tracks and looked at Bill.

"You're not going anywhere," she said. "We've been through this before. You're staying right here. If you go, there won't be anyone to let me know what's happening. And there won't be anybody competent working on this case. You've got to stay and try to keep Creighton and Walder from screwing everything up."

Bill shook his head skeptically.

"That's a pretty tall order," he said.

"Well, consider it an order anyway," Riley said firmly. Then she let a grin change her stern expression. "I'm counting on you. Keep me in the loop."

"Where are you going to go now?" Bill asked.

Riley couldn't help but chuckle.

"I don't exactly know," she said. "It wasn't like Walder offered me a flight back to Quantico in the FBI jet. Don't worry about me, I'll manage. Now get back to work."

Bill nodded and said, "Let me know where you are."

He patted Riley on the shoulder and walked back toward the table. Riley went outside.

At the far end of the parking lot, she saw that a tow truck was taking away Amber Turner's SUV. Her eye was caught by something lying on the ground where the car had been.

A clue maybe?

She broke into a run to see what it was.

CHAPTER TWENTY NINE

Riley saw a small scrap of colorful paper lying on the pavement in the spot where the murdered woman's car had been. Breathless with anticipation, she picked it up and looked at it in the light of a parking lot lamp.

It was a photo that appeared to have been clipped out of a magazine. It showed an old brick mansion with a wraparound porch and stately columns. She pulled out her flashlight to see the image better. If there had been a caption, a story, or a headline, it had been cut away. Riley turned the picture over. A jumble of shapes and partial words looked like they might be part of a magazine ad.

Where could it have come from?

Judging from where it lay on the pavement, Riley thought the picture might well have fallen out of the door to the SUV when Amber Turner's body had been removed by the medical examiner's team.

Or maybe not, she thought.

If it was a clue, had it been left here deliberately or accidentally? And what might it mean?

Her mind raced as she tried to make any kind of meaningful connection between the picture and the murder that had happened on this spot. Then she remembered the note that had arrived by mail in Rhodes' rented room in Philadelphia.

Glad you like the house in the picture. It will suit your purposes well. You'll be expected there very soon.

Was this the house the note had referred to? Was the picture connected to the killer rather than to the victim?

The note had been addressed to Orin Rhodes, but with no clue who had sent it.

Again, Riley felt a creeping worry that it had been Shane Hatcher, and that he had left the picture here, and that he was playing her for a fool. However much she doubted it, she couldn't deny that it was a possibility.

Regardless of who had sent it, where was this house? Was Orin Rhodes staying there right now? How could she find out anything about it?

Riley looked back toward the bar. For a moment, she thought about hurrying back to the meeting and bringing the photo to the team's attention. Maybe together, the agents could figure out what it meant. It was likely that the technicians at Quantico could run down the source of the image.

But she quickly decided that it would be futile. If Walder was still online, he'd just remind her that she was off the case. And if the videoconference had ended, Emily Creighton was now the agent in charge. Creighton would categorically ignore anything Riley brought to her attention.

It was, after all, just a piece of trash in the parking lot.

Riley felt her spirits sinking and despair rising. She knew that part of it was simple exhaustion. In a single day, she had flown from Quantico to Sing Sing, then to Philadelphia, and now here to Florida. She needed a good night's sleep before making any decisions about what to do next.

But then she realized:

Where am I going to spend the night?

She smiled bitterly, admitting that she had no idea. Doubtless, accommodations had been reserved for the team from Quantico. But Riley didn't feel like going back to ask about a room, much less waiting for someone to give her a ride. She remembered that they had driven past a small motel on the way here. It was within walking distance of the sports bar. With luck, there would be some vacancies. This didn't seem like a busy time of the year.

She was also pretty sure that she had spotted a liquor store nearby.

I could really use a drink, Riley thought, as she trudged along the dark road alone.

*

The motel room was shabby and smelled a little musty. But it had a bed and a bathroom and Riley had found the bottle of bourbon she needed. Before she got too settled in, she had a call to make. She was long overdue to touch base with April. Hoping her daughter would still be awake, she got out her laptop and called her for a video chat.

When April answered, she looked and sounded surprisingly cheerful.

"Hey, Mom, what's up?"

Before Riley could reply, she noticed something odd about April's surroundings. It didn't look like the safe house motel room. It looked like she was in a large and attractive room with large windows.

"Where are you?" she asked.

April giggled.

"Well, I guess Dad and I've got some explaining to do," she said. "Hey, Dad, come on over. It's Mom."

In a moment, Ryan's face joined April's on the screen.

"I guess you're wondering what this is all about," Ryan said, smiling.

Riley was starting to panic.

"Where the hell are the two of you?" she asked.

Both Ryan and April looked a bit surprised at her sharp tone.

"Hey, chill out, Mom, there's nothing to get upset about," April said.

"Remember how much April loved Chincoteague when she was little?" Ryan said.

Riley gasped.

"Ryan, please don't tell me that's where you are," she said.

"Come on, Riley," he said. "That place was an insult to April. To all of us."

Riley struggled to collect her wits.

"It was safe," Riley snapped. "Ryan, what in God's name were you thinking? How long have you been there?"

"We just got here," Ryan said. "Listen, Riley, I didn't mean to alarm you. April was feeling so bad about being in that dump. I was trying to be helpful."

"Where are the agents who were guarding her at the safe house?" Riley asked.

"We told the agent on duty that we were leaving," Ryan said.

"You don't have anyone there protecting you?"

"I have this," he replied, holding up a small pistol.

"Cool, huh?" April chimed in.

Riley knew about the gun. Ryan had had it for a few years now. It was a .22-caliber revolver—little more than a toy, as far as Riley was concerned. It certainly wouldn't do Ryan any good against a ruthless killer like Rhodes.

"Have you ever even fired that thing?" she demanded.

"Of course," Ryan snapped. "I'm not stupid. I took the short course, and I was pretty good at it too."

Riley drew a deep breath. Nothing would be gained by fighting with her ex-husband right now. "Does anybody know where you are?" she asked.

"Nope," April said. "Not even the FBI."

"Well, you're going to tell me right now. But nobody else. Do you hear me?"

April rolled her eyes.

"Jeez, OK, Mom. I don't know why you're making such a big deal out of this."

Ryan gave Riley the address, and Riley carefully wrote it down.

Then she said, "I don't want either of you to leave that house."

"Mom," April complained, "we're smart enough not to wander around outside."

"Don't even step outside the door. And stay away from windows."

Ryan was looking embarrassed now.

"I'm sorry, Riley," he said. "We will be careful."

"I've got to go," Riley said. "I'm going to have an agent come out there."

"All right," Ryan replied. "I don't really think it's necessary but if it will make you feel better—"

Riley ended the call. She immediately picked up her phone and dialed Lucy Vargas's number. Lucy sounded surprised to hear from Riley at this hour.

Riley said, "Did you know that April's not at the motel?"

She heard Lucy gasp with disbelief.

"What?" Lucy asked.

"Who was watching her a couple of hours ago at the safe house?"

"It was Darlene Olsen's shift," Lucy said.

Riley remembered Darlene Olsen. Riley had considered her a promising young agent, but now it appeared that she was rather easily duped.

"Lucy, do you know where Chincoteague is?"

"Yes," Lucy said.

"How soon can you get there?"

Lucy fell silent for a moment.

"I've got an assignment first thing tomorrow morning," Lucy said. "If I go tonight, I'll just have to drive right back again. It'll be better for me to send someone else. I'll get in touch with Darlene, tell her to get over there right away."

"Do that," Riley said. "And thanks."

Riley gave Lucy the address and ended the call. Then she sat on the edge of the bed, her mind reeling from Ryan's sheer stupidity. She wished she could go to Chincoteague herself right now. But there was no way she could get there in time to do any good. She hoped that Darlene Olsen would get there in a hurry.

Meanwhile, she desperately needed something to calm her nerves. She was glad she'd bought a bottle of bourbon. She poured herself a glass. But she had barely taken a couple of sips before she got a video chat request.

The call was from Jilly in Phoenix, and Riley answered it cheerfully. Each time she had talked with Jilly, the girl looked healthier than before. It was almost hard to remember the abused and undernourished waif she'd met in Phoenix.

"Hey, Riley," Jilly said.

"Hey, yourself," Riley replied with a smile. "So what's going on?" she asked.

"Nothing much," Jilly said.

Jilly's voice and expression were bored and a bit sullen. Riley wondered what might be wrong. But then, she told herself, Jilly was a young teenager and that was a pretty typical expression.

"Are you ready to go back to school?" Riley asked.

"I'm flunking algebra," Jilly said matter-of-factly.

"What are you going to do about that?"

Jilly popped her bubble gum.

"Study harder, I guess," she said.

"Sounds like you'd better do that."

Jilly lowered her eyes.

"Riley, this just isn't working," Jilly said.

"What's not working?"

"Living here. With the Flaxmans."

Riley's heart sank. She had thought that things were going fine in Jilly's new foster home.

"What's wrong?" Riley asked.

"I don't know," Jilly said with a shrug. "It's just not home, that's all. I'm just a visitor."

After a pause, Jilly added, "I think I'll just go back and live with my dad."

Riley could hardly believe her ears. Jilly's father was drunk and abusive. Child Protective Services had gone to a lot of trouble to get her away from him.

"That's just crazy talk, Jilly."

"Well, at least he's really family."

"No. He's not."

Riley saw Jilly's eyes start to fill up with tears.

"You're right, he's not," Jilly said in a thick voice. "I don't have any family at all. Except …"

"I can't adopt you, Jilly," Riley said.

"Why …"

Jilly's voice trailed off. But Riley knew what she wanted to say. Riley swallowed hard. She and Jilly had had this conversation before. It never ended well.

Riley simply didn't know where to begin. Right now, she had her hands full just trying to keep April safe. After fifteen years, she was only starting to feel like an adequate mother. Trying to raise Jilly would be more of a challenge than she could possibly deal with—especially if she hoped to keep working.

Besides, she was sure that the idea was just a fantasy to Jilly, an escape from reality—even the good reality she now had. Jilly had spent thirteen years feeling hopeless, helpless, and unloved. She'd never learned anything else. Now that she was being cared for by a loving family, she didn't know how to handle it.

Riley knew that she had to be firm.

"You've got to give yourself time with the Flaxmans, sweetie," Riley said, trying to keep her voice under control.

"How long?" Jilly asked.

Tears were pouring down her cheeks now.

"You're in a good place, Jilly," Riley said. "You're with good people. I'm sorry, but you've just got to do your best."

Jilly didn't say anything. She just wiped her eyes.

"I've got to go now," Riley said. "You take care of yourself."

Jilly still didn't say anything. Riley ended the call. She sat there, aching inside.

She took a deep swallow of the bourbon. It burned going down, and it felt wonderful.

Maybe it will help me get some sleep, she thought, as she took several more swallows in a row.

"Happy New Year," she muttered to herself as she felt unconsciousness coming on.

She realized that her dreams were going to take her into some very dark places. She shrugged off the worry. After all, it was just as well. Dark places were exactly where she needed to go right now.

CHAPTER THIRTY

Riley felt a flash of déjà vu. She was engulfed by thick swirling snow and she knew that the storm concealed a terrible threat. She'd been here before. She was sure of it. But she couldn't remember when or how.

Now a shadowy figure was running toward her through the snow. She remembered that too, but couldn't quite say who it was or what was happening. For a moment the snow obscured the figure completely, then it cleared enough to reveal a person whose hand was raised—not in greeting, Riley knew, but pointing a gun directly at her.

Riley drew her own Glock and fired. The figure stopped running but didn't fall. Desperately, Riley fired again, and again, and again …

Then the snow cleared away and everything came to a standstill. Riley found herself facing a pretty, rather awkward-looking girl about April's age.

Riley knew that it was Heidi Wright.

She was bleeding from the bullets Riley had fired. Heidi just stood there and smiled. Then the snow began falling again and the girl began to speak.

"It's no good," the girl said. "You can't kill love. And Orin loves me. I'll always be with him."

The figure twisted and writhed until it morphed into someone else. Now it was Orin Rhodes himself, looking as young as he'd been when Riley had killed his girlfriend.

"Now you know," Orin said, still smiling. "It's all for Heidi. All the killing that I've done, all the killing that's yet to do. Especially yours, Riley Paige. You're going to pay for what you did to her—and to me."

Still smiling, Orin Rhodes slowly turned and walked away into the falling snow.

Riley found herself alone in the blizzard. There was no sign of the girl she had killed or the boy who had declared vengeance. There was no sound except the cold wind.

She called out, hoping someone would hear her—someone who cared and understood.

"Please tell me. Was I wrong? Was what I did so terrible that other people have to die? Do I deserve this?"

Riley felt a strong hand touch her shoulder from behind.

"You did all that you could," a gruff but kindly voice said. "You did exactly what you had to do."

The voice was familiar, at once stern and kindly. It gave Riley tremendous comfort. But when she turned around to face the speaker, no one was there. She saw nothing but whirling snow.

"Come back!" she called out desperately. "Help me!"

Riley awoke in her motel bed with tears pouring down her face. No light was coming through the window, so dawn had not yet come. She remembered every detail of her dream perfectly. And she still felt the same grief, horror, and confusion.

More memories brought more despair—memories of yesterday, and being fired from the case. It finally hit her that it was over—everything she valued and held dear in life. She might as well give up. Even Bill couldn't help her now.

I'm through, she thought, weeping harder now. *At long last, I'm through.*

Worst of all, she was alone.

Then she remembered something else from her dream—that firm but gentle touch, that tough but kindly voice.

"You did all that you could. You did exactly what you had to do."

Who had given her that comfort? Who said those words?

Then she remembered—she hadn't been alone on that fateful day sixteen years ago when she'd shot down Heidi Wright. Someone had been by her side that day and many days afterward. Someone to comfort, nurture, and teach her.

And that *someone* wasn't very far way from her right now.

I've got to go see him, she thought.

She picked up her phone and dialed a number that she hadn't used in a very long time.

144

CHAPTER THIRTY ONE

When she got out of a taxi later that morning in Miami, Riley wondered if she'd come to the right address. Before her stood a tall building that gleamed in the sunlight—hardly the place where she would expect Jake Crivaro to live.

Jake had been her partner and mentor many years ago, when she was just starting her career with the FBI. He was now seventy-five and retired and living here in Miami. But she couldn't imagine him living here, in this towering structure.

On the way from the airport, Riley had kept expecting the driver to exit into one of Miami's suburban neighborhoods. Instead, the driver had kept going until they were winding among tall buildings. Miami itself didn't look like what she'd expected—at least not this part of Miami. It looked like any other major city, high and shiny with glass and metal.

Where are the palm trees?

It was hard to imagine that there were beaches anywhere nearby.

She walked into the building's swank lobby, where a smiling female receptionist stood at a desk.

"May I help you, ma'am?" the woman asked.

Riley was feeling more puzzled by the moment.

"Um, I'm here to visit Jake Crivaro," she said.

"Could I have your name, please?"

"Riley Paige."

The woman looked at a clipboard.

"Oh, yes," she said. "He told me he was expecting you. I'll let him know you're here."

The woman picked up a phone, punched in a number, and said, "Riley Paige is here to visit you, Mr. Crivaro."

The woman nodded at whatever was said in reply, then hung up.

"You may use the elevator, ma'am. His apartment is on the thirty-fifth floor."

Riley rode up in the elevator. When she stepped out of it she was greeted by Jake, who was standing outside his apartment door.

"Hello there, stranger! Happy New Year! Come on in!"

As she walked inside, Riley couldn't help gasping aloud. The apartment was amazing—spacious and modern with lots of glass and sunlight. Riley followed Jake into his living room, with its simple but elegant furniture.

"You look a little dazed," Jake said.

"Yeah, maybe a little," Riley said. "Nothing's quite what I expected."

"I guess you didn't expect a bum like me to be living in a joint like this," he said.

Riley smiled uneasily.

She said, "I wouldn't put it in those words, but—"

"But what? How do you think I managed it?"

Jake stood there with a somewhat wicked-looking smile on his face. She knew he was taunting her, teasing her curiosity. After all, how could anyone live in a place anything like this on an FBI retirement salary?

Riley gulped as a dark possibility occurred to her. Was it possible that Jake had dealt in dirty money? Was that what he was trying to tell her with that devilish grin?

Seeming to guess her thoughts, Jake chuckled.

"Relax, it's totally legit. My son is in real estate here in Miami. He bought the apartment, said it was a good investment. I get to live here, and I've only got to pay the maintenance fees. It suits me fine."

Riley smiled, feeling more comfortable now. Jake led Riley through sliding glass doors out onto a narrow balcony. In one direction were more glass buildings. In the other direction she could see water, bridges, and the barrier islands that she knew must include Miami Beach.

"Nice view of Biscayne Bay, huh?" Jake said. "Great beaches are right out there. Not that I go over there much. I've got everything I need right here—a great pool, exercise facilities. And I'm right downtown, so there's plenty to do."

Riley stood basking in the warm Miami air. It was hard to believe that only yesterday morning she'd been shivering in the cold of Upstate New York.

Jake himself was certainly a sight for sore eyes—a short, barrel-chested man who managed to look both tough and dapper. She'd last seen him briefly a few months ago at a parole hearing. Then they were both revisiting the case that had prompted Jake into an angry, bitter retirement.

When she'd seen him, he'd grumbled about hip and knee replacements, eye problems, a hearing aid, and a pacemaker.

But to look at him now, Riley wouldn't guess there was anything wrong with him. He looked younger than his seventy-five years, and scarcely less energetic than he had when they'd worked together years ago.

With a look of concern, he said, "You're not doing so good, are you?"

Riley smiled wanly.

"How'd you guess?" she said.

"Come on, kid. This is Jake you're talking to. I've got instincts. Not as good as the instincts you've acquired over the years—I always knew you'd get better than me sooner or later. But my instincts will still do in a pinch."

He guided her back into the apartment.

"Let's talk about it over lunch," he said.

*

A little while later, Riley was sitting with Jake at his dining area table. They were finishing the sandwiches he'd made. She had just brought him up to date on the Orin Rhodes case, and how she'd been taken off of it. She held back no facts or details—not even her unsettling communications with Shane Hatcher.

Jake was visibly shocked as Riley described Rhodes' attack on April and the two sadistic killings that followed.

"Jesus, I'd never have thought it," he said. "The kid we put away seemed so repentant. And I kept hearing what a model prisoner he'd been over the years. So it was all just an act to get early release. He sure fooled us all but good."

Jake sat there for a moment, trying to take it all in.

"And now you've gone rogue," he finally said. "I know what that's like. I was at odds with the powers-that-be at the Bureau more than a few times. Sometimes you've got to buck the system if you really want to get the job done."

He leaned toward her, gazing at her thoughtfully.

"But you haven't told me everything, have you?" he said. "And I'm not talking just about the case. I'm talking about *you*."

Riley felt a surge of the despair she'd been struggling with since last night. She remembered images from her dream—of Heidi Wright riddled with bullets, and how she'd said:

"You can't kill love."

And then Heidi morphing into Orin Rhodes, who'd said:

"It's all for Heidi."

Riley struggled with her thoughts and feelings.

"I'm having some ugly thoughts, Jake," she said. "Like this whole thing is my fault somehow."

She waited for a moment for Jake to tell her how crazy that was. He didn't say anything.

She said, "It started with me, Jake. I killed her. I know, I *had* to kill her, but that doesn't change the fact that I *did* kill her. I'm not prepared to deal with this. I'm not strong enough to face Orin Rhodes. He's got revenge driving his every move. But all I've got is … guilt. I feel too weak."

Jake scratched his chin thoughtfully.

"Shut your eyes for a minute, Riley," he said.

Riley knew what was coming next—or at least she thought she did. She was known in the Bureau for her ability to get into a killer's skin, to find her way into the darkness of his mind. She'd learned this skill from Jake. As good as he'd been at it in his own time, she knew that she'd surpassed him long ago.

Riley shut her eyes.

Jake asked, "Did you ever kill somebody you really and truly wanted to kill?"

Riley was a bit surprised by the question. But she knew the answer without stopping to think.

"Yes," she said.

The last person she had truly wanted to kill was Peterson—the sadistic monster who had caged and tormented both her and April. And she had felt an almost terrifying satisfaction in his death.

"Remember that time," Jake said. "Remember what it was like."

The memory came back in a flood of images.

She was trapped under a house in the dark, shrinking back from a flame that moved toward her. She heard Peterson's ugly laugh. But then something changed. It wasn't Riley who was being tortured anymore. Instead, Peterson was tormenting her friend Marie with the flame, and Riley could do nothing to stop him. She knew that Marie was already dead, but she clawed through the darkness toward the deadly light anyhow.

When she got closer she saw that it was April crying out and shrinking away from the fire. April was struggling to escape the man who had tormented Marie until she killed herself, who had tortured Riley until she managed to escape.

Then the darkness overcame them all, and the scene changed.

Riley was on the bank of a river, and Peterson was holding April, bound hand and foot, out in the water. April had fought back, but she was about to drown in the freezing water. Riley moved forward with a murderous determination she had seldom found in herself. She lifted a sharp heavy rock and knocked the man down to the water with a strike to the head. Then she struck him again and again, crushing his face with the rock as the river turned red with blood.

"How did it feel?" Jake asked.

Riley realized that she'd been describing the vision aloud.

"Wonderful," she said, her eyes still closed.

"You're getting the idea," Jake said.

Yes, I'm getting the idea, Riley thought.

It was easy now to connect with Orin Rhodes' mind. All she had to do was imagine killing Peterson in a different manner. She pictured herself in the river again. This time she thought about Orin Rhodes as he had killed Kirby Steadman in South Carolina.

Riley stood facing the man, knee-deep in cold river water. But this time she was holding her Glock with a full clip of ammo. She was Orin Rhodes now.

She fired one shot into Peterson's shoulder and watched him staggering toward the shore, trying to get away.

Delighting in her adversary's pain and terror, Riley fired another shot, and then another, and then another ...

Riley's eyes snapped open. Jake was gazing at her with an expression of complete understanding.

"You know what it's all about now, don't you?" he said.

"Yes," Riley said.

After all, her own dark lust for revenge had really been no different from Orin Rhodes'.

"And do you still feel weak and unprepared?" Jake asked.

Riley shook her head no.

Jake smiled.

"Good," he said. "Now let's get to work."

CHAPTER THIRTY TWO

Riley suddenly felt renewed and energized, ready to focus on the case with white-hot intensity. She could tell by Jake's grin that he shared her excitement.

"So what have you got in the way of evidence?" he asked.

"I'm still trying to make sense of a couple of things," Riley said.

She handed Jake the message that she and Bill had found at Rhodes' room.

"Bill and I found this when we checked out a room that Rhodes had rented in Philadelphia. Somebody sent it to Rhodes by regular mail."

Jake read a bit of the message aloud.

"'*Glad you like the house in the picture.*' What picture is that?"

"Bill and I had no idea," Riley said. "There wasn't a picture in the envelope. But last night, I found this in the parking lot where Amber Turner was killed. I haven't sent it to Quantico to be located because I'm off the case and it's probably not relevant anyhow. Still, I have a feeling about it."

She handed him the cut-out magazine photo.

"It looks vaguely familiar," Jake said. "I think I've seen this somewhere before."

"Think, Jake! Where could it be?"

He turned the image from side to side. Finally he said, "I can't place it. But those are mangrove trees there in the background. Lots of those out in the Everglades."

Riley felt a jolt of excitement. She said, "Rhodes left fliers about the Everglades in his cabin back in South Carolina. There's got to be some kind of connection."

"Let me see what I can find out."

Jake opened his computer and muttered softly to himself as he did some quick searches.

"Not there. But maybe in a file of abandoned properties that a buddy once showed me."

He located a particular website and scrolled through the images.

"There it is!" Riley cried.

Jake clicked the image and it came up larger on his monitor. He leaned closer and read the text.

"Yep. It's an abandoned house out in the Everglades."

"It's in the national park?" Riley asked.

"It was built before the Everglades was a national park. There are other places like this around Florida, abandoned mansions that belonged to powerful criminals before their dirty deals finally caught up with them. This one belonged to a mafia don back in the day—Fingers Lucanza, I think they called him."

Jake sat back in his chair and grinned. "An old pal of mine is the chief ranger in the park—Wilbur Strait's his name. He told me about this place and showed me a picture of it. I'd forgotten all about it."

Riley felt ready to boil over with excitement.

"That's where Rhodes is, Jake! We've got three clues that say so—the letter he got in Philadelphia, the fliers about the Everglades, and now this picture. He's hiding in that abandoned mansion. We've got to go there right now!"

Jake chuckled at Riley's impatience. "Now slow down just a little. We haven't proved anything yet. Before we go in there half-cocked, let's check this out. Let's get Wilbur on the phone."

Jake called up his friend, the chief ranger in the Everglades. He put his phone on speaker so that Riley could listen and talk. After Jake and Wilbur Strait exchanged greetings, Jake got right to the point.

"Wilbur, I'm sitting here with a friend from the FBI. She and I both think maybe some bad guy might be hiding out in the old Fingers Lucanza mansion. Have you got any reason to think that yourself?"

Wilbur Strait thought for a moment.

"I don't know about that exactly," he said. "But we do have a situation here. A hiker disappeared a couple of days back—on Tuesday. We haven't been able to find the guy anywhere. He was out exploring the park all alone so I guess he could have been taken by a gator, but his friends say he's an experienced outdoorsman."

It sounded to Riley as though Orin Rhodes had claimed another victim. She decided to get into the conversation.

"Chief Strait, my name's Riley Paige, and—"

Strait interrupted.

"Wait a minute. Did you say Riley Paige?"

"Yes. Why?"

"Well, I'll be damned. Somebody called our switchboard, must have been the day the hiker disappeared. The guy kept saying, 'Tell Riley Paige that she'd better watch her step.' We had no idea who Riley Paige was. We figured somebody must have gotten the wrong number."

Riley and Jake locked gazes. She knew they were thinking the same thing. The anonymous caller was surely Shane Hatcher, calling in just as he had after Rhodes' two murders. He was still on Rhodes' trail. Or he was still working with Rhodes. Riley couldn't be sure which was true.

Riley said, "Chief Strait, the man we're looking for is named Orin Rhodes. He's armed and extremely dangerous. He's killed at least two people within the last few days. And if he's hiding in that mansion, we need to get him. What are the chances of us putting together a team to storm the mansion, SWAT-style?"

Strait replied in a confident tone.

"I've got some rangers here who'd be up to it. And we could bring in a few local cops who've been through SWAT training."

Riley asked Jake, "How long will it take us to drive to the Everglades location?"

"A couple of hours," he replied.

Riley said, "Chief Strait, do you think you can get your team together in time to get out there today?"

"Sure," Strait said. "It will be getting late in the day but we should be able to get out there before dark."

Riley's cell phone buzzed. She saw that the call was from Bill.

"I've got to take this," she told Jake and the chief ranger. "You two firm up your plans."

Riley got up and walked out onto the balcony, where she took Bill's call.

"Things are a real mess here, Riley," Bill said. "Creighton and Huang are interviewing everybody in Apex who knew Amber Turner—family, friends, co-workers, the works. They're turning up nothing. The girl had no prior connection to Rhodes. Both killings so far have been random, just like you've been saying."

"I'm not surprised," Riley said.

Bill continued, "The problem is, Creighton just won't give up. She's sure she'll find out something if she interviews absolutely everybody. She's driving the town crazy, and she's on the verge of causing a local panic. She's got people thinking that any of them might be the killer's next target."

Riley groaned a little. Bill was right—things really were a mess.

"So what are you going to do?" Riley asked.

"I'm at the airport," Bill said. "I'm flying back to Quantico. Walder won't listen to reason, but Meredith might. But this isn't something I can sort out on video chat. I've got to take care of it in person. And I'm going to do my damnedest to get you back on the case."

Riley felt breathless with excitement.

"Actually, I *am* on the case," she said. "And I think I've got something. I'm visiting Jake Crivaro in Miami. We're all but sure that Rhodes is holed up in an old mansion in the Everglades. Hatcher's also in the area. Jake and I are going to drive there right now. We're joining up with an assault team that the chief ranger's putting together."

Bill fell silent for a moment.

"Is there a place for the FBI jet to land in that area?" he asked.

"Let me check," Riley said. She poked her head back in the door and asked Jake, "Has the Everglades got an airport?"

Still talking to Chief Strait, Jake nodded.

"Yes," Riley told Bill.

"Great. I'll meet you there."

She and Bill ended the call. Riley stood on the balcony for a moment, staring out over Miami and collecting her thoughts. Picking up Bill would add a little time to the trip, but she was sure that she could use his help.

Is this really happening? she asked herself. *Are we really closing in on Rhodes?*

A lot of risk and effort were going to go into the coming raid. Riley knew she'd better be right.

CHAPTER THIRTY THREE

Riley's nerves grew ever more taut as the large SUV took her deep into the Everglades. She was sure that something big was about to happen. She hoped Orin Rhodes' reign of terror would soon be over.

She was riding with Jake Crivaro and several rangers and cops, all of them wearing Kevlar vests. Chief Ranger Wilbur Strait was driving. Another SUV right behind them carried more well-equipped cops and rangers.

The road followed a waterway through low scrubby jungle. A white pelican took flight up ahead, and Riley realized that under other circumstances, she'd consider the trip quite scenic. She recognized bamboo growing along the water, but wasn't sure about the rest of the tangled thicket. Then, in the late afternoon light she spotted the ominous eyes of alligators watching the passing vehicles from the waterway. She could understand how a solitary hiker might disappear out here.

The two vehicles pulled up to the airport just as the FBI jet taxied to a stop. The side door of the plane opened and Bill came trotting down the steps onto the steaming hot tarmac. He had his own Kevlar vest slung over his shoulder.

Riley rushed toward him.

"Glad you could make it," she said.

Bill grinned at her and patted her on the shoulder.

"Wouldn't miss it for the world," he said.

They climbed into the SUV. As Chief Strait put the vehicle into gear and drove, Riley hastily introduced Jake to Bill. The two men had heard about each other from Riley, but had never actually met. She thought they looked each other over approvingly.

Riley felt good about having both Jake and Bill by her side. They were the two most important people she'd ever worked with in her career. And now here the three of them were, working together. It felt right.

While Bill was putting on his vest, Riley got out the picture of the house they were going to. He took the photo and pulled out his flashlight to study it.

"Remember the note that someone sent to Rhodes in Philadelphia?" she said.

"You think this is the house?"

"It could be. I found that in the parking lot in Jacksonville. And in South Carolina he had been looking at information on the Everglades.

Bill nodded slowly. "It sure sounds like we've got him," he finally said.

"I hope so," Riley said.

After a few minutes, Chief Strait said, "It's coming right up."

Strait soon pulled the vehicle to a stop at a private side road that had been chained off and fastened with a lock. He got out of the car and cut the chain with a bolt cutter. Then he got back in the car and drove. The SUV rocked and lurched along an overgrown dirt road.

"It doesn't look like anybody has driven this way in a long while," Riley said.

"A lot of folks get around out here by airboat instead of cars," Chief Strait said.

Finally the SUV came within sight of the mansion. Chief Strait stopped the vehicle and cut off the headlights. The other SUV stopped right behind him. The whole improvised ten-member team climbed out.

It was dusk now. She could barely see the large dark snake that slithered across the path in front of them.

Chief Strait led the way, followed by Bill, Riley, and Jake, and then by the others. As they silently approached the mansion, Riley saw that it lay next to a waterway. Rhodes could indeed have come here by airboat. Perhaps one was hidden somewhere in the thick vegetation.

Riley was sweating now. She realized that it was more from nerves than from the cooling tropical temperature. Her flashlight caught a motion at the water's edge and revealed alligators that had been disturbed at the strangers' approach. One opened its wide toothy mouth, and then they all slowly slid into the water.

Chief Strait gathered his team members together, and they broke apart and headed to prearranged positions around the house. Even in the near darkness she could see that it was definitely the mansion she'd seen in the photo—red brick and surrounded by a porch with white columns. It looked larger and more decrepit than it had in the picture, a hollowed-out ruin with many of its huge windows broken.

With its haunted aura, the place gripped Riley's imagination. How long had it been since it had been filled with family members and well-dressed gangsters? How many criminal plans had been laid here? How many murders had been committed on these very premises?

Orin Rhodes must feel perfectly at home, Riley thought.

She could see no lights on inside the building now. That didn't mean he wasn't hiding somewhere inside.

Strait handed Riley a bullhorn. She lifted it and called out, "Orin Rhodes, this is Special Agent Riley Paige, FBI. We've got the house surrounded. Come out through the front door with your hands as high as you can get them."

Her command echoed through the vacant house and the surrounding forest. No reply came. Riley wasn't surprised. But she had no idea what to expect next. Was Orin Rhodes alone in there, or did he have accomplices waiting in ambush? Might Shane Hatcher be in there as well?

Riley called out again, "I repeat. Come out with your hands up."

Again came no reply. Riley, Bill, and Chief Strait exchanged looks and drew their weapons. The three of them had planned ahead of time to be the ones to enter the mansion if necessary. The other members of the team would wait outside to prevent anyone from escaping. But as the three started walking toward the broad porch, Jake Crivaro scurried along with them, smiling impishly at Riley.

Riley felt a flash of worry. This hadn't been part of the plan. Was it a good idea for Jake to join them, with his bad knees, bad eyes, hearing aid, and pacemaker?

Now's no time to argue, Riley thought.

Besides, she understood how Jake must feel. After years of retirement, he wasn't going to stay on the sidelines. He was eager for some action. Riley couldn't blame him.

With Riley in the lead, the group pushed through the double front doors that hung ajar. Holding their guns and flashlights up in front of them, they checked inside each opening as they moved through a wide hallway.

Then they stood still and listened. No sound revealed other life within the house. The place seemed even larger, more awe-inspiring than it had from the outside.

Chief Strait said softly, "We need to get a better look at these rooms."

The three men separated to check them out. Riley turned her flashlight on a circular stairway that wound upward to a gallery. She climbed upward.

At the top of the stairs she moved quietly along a balcony, then encountered a pair of double doors. She pushed a door open

156

carefully and stepped into an enormous room. It was flanked by tall windows that were dark now. Then her roving light caught something right in the center of the space.

Riley stood still and kept her light on the object. It was a single straight-back chair facing away from Riley. Someone was sitting there. It looked like a man, and his head was tilted awkwardly to one side.

"Orin Rhodes?" Riley said sharply.

But she already sensed that this wasn't Orin Rhodes. The room was filled with a familiar ugly stench. Whoever was sitting in that chair had been dead for days.

She flashed her light around the room again to make sure no one else was there. Then she yelled to her companions downstairs, "I've got something up here."

As she heard footsteps coming up the steps, Riley walked around in front of the chair. A man was sitting there. His eyes and mouth were all wide open. Judging from the smell and skin discoloration, he had been dead for at least two days. Like the corpses in South Carolina and the town of Apex, this body was riddled with bullets.

Riley almost gagged on the stench. She had no doubt that she'd found the missing hiker. This man hadn't been taken by a gator. He hadn't fallen prey to any wildlife that was natural to this wilderness. He had become yet another random victim of a madman.

But where is Orin Rhodes? she wondered.

Riley was holding a handkerchief over her face, examining the body more closely when Bill, Jake, and Chief Strait joined her.

"Does it look like he was killed right here?" Chief Strait asked.

Riley considered it a good question. How strictly was Rhodes sticking to his MO? She pointed out details and began to explain.

"Rhodes normally likes to torment his victims, make them plead and try to escape. But there's no blood around the chair and no trail of blood leading here. He wasn't killed here."

Jake pointed to the body as well.

"His clothes are torn and stained," Jake said. "Rhodes chased him outdoors until firing the final shot to his forehead."

"That's right," Riley said. "Then Rhodes brought the body up here. The hiker was a smallish man, so Rhodes could have done that by himself."

Riley looked around. She saw no evidence that Rhodes had spent much time here. But of course, that meant little. She remembered how thoroughly he'd cleaned out the cabin in South Carolina before leaving.

Bill reached for the victim's jacket pocket.

"Here's something," he said.

He pulled an envelope out of the pocket. It had no name written on it, but Riley knew that the message inside was meant for her.

Bill seemed to realize this too. He handed the envelope to her, and she opened it. Written on a plain piece of paper in Rhodes' familiar printing was an extremely short message.

You lose!
If you come alone she might still be alive.

Bill, Jake, and Chief Strait stood looking at the note in her hand.

"What the hell is that supposed to mean?" Jake asked.

Riley said nothing. But the meaning of the words was absolutely clear to her. Orin Rhodes had played her into being in the wrong place at the wrong time. He had lured her as far away from her home as possible.

Because April was the real target all along.

CHAPTER THIRTY FOUR

It was cold outside, but April loved the view from the third-story balcony. She and Daddy really had picked out a wonderful house to rent in Chincoteague. It was three stories tall, and it had many rooms and lots of balconies and porches that looked out over the water.

Of course, April knew that she wasn't supposed to be out here. She was under strict orders to stay inside and away from windows. But Darlene, the agent whose job it was to protect her, was in the kitchen making a snack. And Daddy was somewhere else in the house, working on a legal case on his computer.

Some "vacation," she thought.

She should have known that Daddy couldn't leave his work behind even for just a day or two.

Not that she cared very much. Nobody would notice if she came out here for just a few minutes. She thought it would be a shame to come all the way to Chincoteague and not enjoy the view. And it really was a wonderful view, overlooking the waterfront of the Assateague Channel.

She'd found a pair of binoculars lying around in the house. She was looking through them at Assateague Island, right across the channel. That was where herds of wild ponies lived. She could see them right now, a small group of mixed dark and pintos. They were beautiful.

She thought back fondly to when Dad and Mom had brought her here when she was little. It had been summer, and there was a lot more to see and do back then. She'd gotten to watch the pony roundup. Every summer, 150 adult wild ponies and the foals that were born in the spring swam the channel over here to Chincoteague Island.

She smiled as she remembered how she'd cried when the ponies were auctioned off, and Mom and Dad said she couldn't have one. Of course, she now understood that it was the right decision. But back then she'd been too little to understand.

She tilted the binoculars down to look along the shore on their side of the channel. She saw some pretty white birds. But as she swept the binoculars along the beach, something fleetingly caught her eye—a man in a jacket, she thought. Or were her eyes just playing tricks on her? She moved the binoculars back and forth, trying to find him again. She was interrupted by the glass doors sliding open behind her.

"April! What are you doing out here!"

April lowered the binoculars. It was Darlene, looking none too happy with her.

April pointed down at the beach.

"Darlene!" she said. "I saw somebody down there!"

She handed the binoculars to Darlene, who surveyed the beach.

"I don't see anybody," Darlene said.

April leaned over the rail and looked carefully. Now she couldn't see anybody either.

"Come on, get back inside," Darlene said.

"But Darlene—"

"That's an order!"

April and Darlene went back inside. April wanted to think that the man was just a trick of the light, a figment of her imagination.

But the image was still there, like a sudden quick flash of light that kept flickering in the retina even after it was gone. The man had been real, all right. And April felt sure that he'd been looking up at her.

*

Orin Rhodes stood looking up at the lights inside the elegant vacation home. The father and the daughter were in there, relaxing and taking it easy.

They've got no idea what they're in for, he thought.

He'd seen the girl just this afternoon. She'd been standing on the upstairs balcony, looking around with binoculars. Then a woman had come out and taken the girl back inside—an FBI agent, no doubt.

Orin wasn't worried about her. He was sure he could handle her. And he hadn't spotted any other agents through the windows, or any watching in cars. He'd already used his laptop computer to find out that the house had no security system. The whole thing was going to be almost too easy.

Although the night was cold, Orin felt a warm swell of self-satisfaction. He'd played his hand perfectly every step of the way so far. It had been especially smart of him to hire that cheap private eye to follow Ryan Paige's movements. That's how he had found out that the girl was being kept under guard in the motel.

Attacking there and then had been out of the question. The last thing he'd wanted was an open firefight with the FBI. So he'd been patient. And soon his patience had paid off. The private eye had seen the girl and her father leave the motel and had followed them here.

The detective had dutifully given Orin the address, and Orin had paid him for completing the job. Now Orin was so happy with the detective's work that he decided not to kill him after all.

But what about Riley Paige? he wondered.

What was she doing right now?

He'd certainly led her on a long chase through South Carolina and Florida. The two murders had been big, flashy statements, and she hadn't ignored them. He had successfully lured her far away from her family. But had she picked up on the more subtle clues?

For example, the "message" he had mailed to himself in Philadelphia? The fliers for the Everglades that he'd left in the cabin in South Carolina? And what about the cut-out picture of the mansion in the Everglades?

Finally, what about the note he had left on the body in the mansion? Surely she'd understand it if she saw it. Surely she'd damn well keep quiet and come here by herself, with no backup of any kind.

In fact, if all had gone perfectly, she might well be on her way here right now. But he knew better than to expect too much from chance. Chance had dealt him a lucky hand so far, and he knew that his luck wouldn't last forever. If need be, a simple phone call would be enough to lure Riley Paige into the trap he was setting for her right now.

She'd suffer before she died, and Heidi would be avenged. And then Heidi's spirit would be free, and Orin would be free as well. He could kill randomly and viciously to his heart's content for as long as chance would allow.

Life is good, he thought. *And death is good too.*

Orin looked up and down the beach. No other houses were close to this one, and there was no activity in the neighborhood.

The lights were brightest in the second floor of the house. That must be the main floor. Yes, he could see nice outside stairs going up to the double-door main entrance. A few lights showed on the third floor, which he was sure must be made up of bedrooms.

The first floor was completely dark, which suited him well. That part of the house was probably entirely garage and storage areas. It was going to be the perfect place to break in without being noticed.

He was surveying the house from just beyond the patch of light thrown by a fixture over the garage. A door off to one side looked promising. He figured it must have a deadbolt lock, but that wouldn't hold him up long.

He moved quickly across the lighted area to the doorway. Then he fished a couple of bobby pins out of his pocket. He'd learned how to use them from a burglar pal in prison. The pins were already bent to just the angles he needed.

Standing exposed in the light like this might be the most dangerous part of this undertaking. But he couldn't let that rattle him. He slowed down his breathing to calm his nerves.

Inserting one bent bobby pin into the lock as a tension wrench, he inserted the other above it, then slid it toward him, teasing the pins lightly. It took him three tries, but soon he was able to twist the bolt free.

He pushed the door open silently, then shut it behind him. The room was dark, and it was a relief to be out of the light. He stood and listened for a moment. As he expected, the door wasn't wired for an alarm, and no one seemed to have heard him lightly scratching the lock.

He took the pistol out of his jacket and attached the suppressor to it. Then he surveyed his surroundings with a small flashlight. He was in a large storage room. A couple of kayaks lay across supports, and their paddles were hanging on the wall. There were dozens of boxes on metal shelves—doubtless everything one could want for a vacation on the water.

A faint sliver of light came from beneath the door on the other side of the room. He opened it slowly and saw that it led into a hallway. A stairway went up to a landing and then turned out of sight.

Before he could start on his way up the stairs, he heard a sound from above—a door opening, he thought. Had someone heard him after all? Or was this just a routine late-night check of the premises?

A light turned on over the stairway, and he backed into the shadows under the stairs. The footsteps sounded light—the woman or the girl, Orin suspected. Then she came into view on the landing—the woman he had thought to be an FBI agent. She looked young and inexperienced, relaxed and unwary as she came down the stairs on what she must have thought was a routine check. She hadn't even drawn her gun from the holster on her hip.

He was briefly tempted to torment her with bullets as he had the others. But no, this killing had to be quick and efficient. It was purely a practical matter. Gratification must come later.

He stepped out of the shadows and raised his gun. Time slowed down as she turned her head to see him. Her mouth fell open with surprise, but before she could utter a sound he fired a round straight into her forehead.

Her eyes wide, she wobbled on her feet for a moment without falling. Then she tottered forward, and he was able to dart toward her and catch her in his arms. He lowered her silently onto the stairs and listened.

Had anyone heard the muffled shot?

If they had, he was ready.

If they didn't, even better!

His gun ready, he climbed up the stairs toward his unsuspecting prey.

CHAPTER THIRTY FIVE

April was playing a game on her laptop when she heard footsteps in the hallway behind her. A moment ago, Darlene had gone out that way to take a routine look around downstairs.

"How's everything, Darlene?" she asked, without bothering to look around.

When no reply came, she turned around and saw a man standing in the open doorway.

She knew who it was. She could never forget that face. He'd made himself look different, with darker hair and some stubble on his chin. But she could never forget those cold, malicious eyes—not after he'd tried to kill her back in Fredericksburg.

She jumped to her feet. Panicked thoughts crowded through her brain.

How could this be? Her mother had flown south, first to South Carolina and now to Florida, in hot pursuit of this same man.

This can't be real.

But after a few stunned seconds, she realized that this was real—and that the man had a gun at his side.

April turned toward her father, who was in the same room watching sports on TV.

"Daddy!" April screamed.

April's father turned his head, gaping in disbelief upon seeing the intruder. April could tell that he hadn't even begun to grasp the danger they were in.

He stood and asked, "Where is Agent Olsen?"

He sounded more indignant than alarmed.

The man sneered and chuckled, flaunting his gun.

"You killed her!" April cried. "You killed Darlene!"

The man shrugged, as if out of modesty.

"As chance would have it—yes, I did," he said.

Then he lifted the gun and pointed it at April's father.

No, April thought. *I can't let him kill Daddy.*

She picked up her laptop, reared back with it, then hurled it as hard as she could at the man. He ducked, and it barely missed his head. Then he whirled around to face her.

"Huh-uh, baby," he said. "You're not getting the best of me this time."

As he started to raise his gun toward her, April dived behind a stuffed chair. She actually felt the wind that the bullet made passing her shoulder. She gasped. She'd been physically attacked more than once, but she'd never been shot at before. She knew that he wasn't aiming to kill her—at least not yet. She'd already be dead if he'd wanted her to be.

Still, the idea of being shot at really pissed her off.

From her position on the floor, she could see her father creeping across the floor toward his briefcase. She knew that was where he kept his own large and menacing pistol.

Why couldn't he have had it handier? she thought.

Regardless, she knew that she had to keep the attacker distracted long enough for Daddy to get his weapon. She threw her whole body against the chair in front of her, knocking it over. The man turned to look at her.

Standing square in front of him and risking a bullet, April reached for a large vase sitting on a stand. She picked it up and threw it at him. He bent down, and the vase flew over his back, then crashed into the floor and burst into pieces.

The distraction had been just enough to allow April's father to open the briefcase and pull out his pistol. April thought it looked pretty small and pitiful in comparison to the gun the man was wielding. And Daddy didn't look at all confident with it. His hands were shaking as he tried to take aim.

But the man's attention was still on April. He didn't seem to have noticed what Daddy was up to. April had to keep it that way. She yanked a large framed picture off the wall, rushed toward the man, and swung it. She successfully knocked the gun out of his hand, and it skidded across the carpet.

He was glaring at her, not at her father. April stared back, holding her breath, hoping that her father would seize his opportunity and blow the man away.

*

Orin kept his eyes on the girl as he backed toward where the gun had fallen. He knew from the last time he attacked her that she was feisty, smart, and brave. It was going to be fun to bring her down at last.

Before he could reach his weapon, he heard a shot ring out, followed by the thud of a bullet entering the wall behind him. He whirled around. Sure enough, the girl's father had a gun of his own—a measly little .22-caliber pistol. He was pointing at Rhodes, gathering his nerves to take another shot.

But he looked much more frightened than Orin felt.

In fact, Orin wasn't scared at all.

He could see in the man's eyes that he didn't have what it took to shoot someone, whether fatally or otherwise. No, the girl's father wasn't the least bit like Orin. He was too timid, too cowardly. Orin guessed that he'd inflicted plenty of emotional pain in his life, and that he was a bully in his way. But he wasn't the kind of bully who had the stomach to inflict actual physical pain, much less really kill someone.

Orin broke into a merry, jig-like dance. The father fired a shot that missed him wide, then another, then another. Orin was laughing now, feeling as safe as if no one was shooting at him at all.

The father's aim grew more erratic. Orin's only worry was that he'd accidentally shoot and kill his own daughter, spoiling Orin's plans for revenge. Orin counted five shots, then abruptly rushed toward the man. He snatched the gun out of his hand and pointed it back at him. Keeping the man in his sights, he began to move toward where his own weapon had fallen.

Then he heard the girl screeching behind him, and she was suddenly pummeling him from behind with her fists. The hits came hard and fierce. He shook her off, then turned and fired a shot that deliberately missed her, but only barely. He knew it was the last bullet in the .22.

The girl took a step backward, giving Orin the chance to get to his own gun and pick it up. Then he raised his weapon and aimed it—not at the girl but directly at her father's head. The girl gasped and backed away, in terror for her father's safety.

Holding the man's empty revolver in his left hand, he rushed forward and slammed the butt into the side of the girl's head. It was a hard blow, but not hard enough to knock her completely out. All he wanted to do was subdue her.

And he could see that he'd succeeded. She staggered, but her gaze was still locked on his, and still defiant. Even so, she was dazed enough now not to be a threat, at least for a few moments. And a few moments was all he needed.

He threw the empty revolver aside, brandishing his own much more formidable CZ P-09 semiautomatic. He quickly removed the suppressor. He wasn't worried about noise anymore, not in this out-of-the-way place. Noise would add spice to the pain and terror he was going to inflict.

Swinging his gun back and forth between father and daughter, he motioned April and Ryan toward a pair of straight-back chairs.

"The two of you—sit right there," he said.

April made a threatening move, but Orin pointed his gun at her father.

"Don't even think about it," he said. "Sit."

They both obeyed. With his free hand, Orin reached into his jacket pocket for his roll of duct tape. His next task was to bind them to the chairs.

But then what?

His revenge wouldn't be complete if Riley Paige didn't get here. He was starting to doubt that she was really on her way at all. Fortunately, he'd had her cell phone number for quite some time. She was just a phone call away.

First, though, he had to immobilize his victims. He couldn't leave that girl loose for long. Still holding the gun in one hand, he pulled a length of tape loose with his teeth.

In a tone of mock hospitality, he said, "I want you both to make yourselves comfortable. This is going to take a long time."

CHAPTER THIRTY SIX

Riley climbed into the driver's seat of the car she had just commandeered at the military airport near Chincoteague. But before Bill could get in the passenger side, she snapped all the doors locked. Bill's mouth dropped open with shock as he stared through the window at her.

She hated to do this to Bill. As soon as they'd found Orin Rhodes' warning on the dead man's body in the Everglades, Bill had pulled every string he could to fly them both back here right away.

Rhodes had warned Riley not to tell anybody of his impending attack on her daughter and ex-husband. It was a warning that both Bill and Riley had taken seriously. That was why they hadn't called in a SWAT team.

Bill hurried around to the driver's window. Riley opened it just a crack.

"What the hell do you think you're doing?" Bill said. "I've got to come with you!"

"You can't, Bill. I'm sorry, but you can't. If we were dealing with any ordinary killer, we could go in together. But Rhodes isn't ordinary. We underestimated him. He sent us on a wild goose chase just so he could get to April. And now he really will kill her if I don't come alone."

"But he doesn't have to know," Bill said.

Riley shook her head miserably.

"He *will* know, Bill. He's been predicting my every move since this whole thing began."

Before Bill could protest further, Riley rolled up her window and drove away. She knew Bill would try to follow her. But first he'd have to get his hands on another car to use. Also, she hadn't told him the exact address where April and Ryan had gone. He could find out by calling Quantico, but that would take some time. She hoped she had enough time to resolve this horrible situation by herself.

As soon as she was on the highway, her cell phone rang. She accepted the call and heard a voice that was full of mockery and contempt.

"Riley Paige, as I live and breathe! How long has it been since we've talked? Why, sixteen long years, I believe! And then it wasn't under the happiest circumstances. We've got so much making up to do. Where are you? I've been expecting you."

"Are they alive?" she demanded.

"Of course," he replied. "We're all just sitting here together. Waiting for you. How soon do you expect to arrive?"

Riley bit her tongue. She knew that she mustn't tell him that she was only a few minutes away from him. For all he knew, she was still back in Florida. She needed to keep him in the dark.

"Well?" he said. "Don't you have anything to tell me?"

Riley felt a tsunami of emotion at his jeering tone. But to her surprise, the emotion wasn't dread or fear. She wasn't going to allow herself to be frightened. For too long, she'd tried to understand this man and his grief for his girlfriend. She'd even tried to empathize with him. And somewhere inside, she'd blamed herself for the monster he'd become.

But those feelings were gone now. The emotion that was sweeping through her now went far beyond anger. It even went beyond Orin Rhodes. She felt blind fury toward every single monster she'd ever hunted down, especially those who had tormented her and the people she loved.

She'd had enough of it. Orin Rhodes was going to experience the full weight of years of pent-up fury. She was filled with raging bloodlust, the likes of which she'd never felt before.

She began to speak in a low, murderous growl.

"Listen to me, you pathetic little bastard. You like other people's pain, don't you? You like the way bullets hurt. You like to take your time. But believe me, you've got no idea what the word *pain* even means. You're going to find out, though. And I'm not using bullets. I'm going to hack you limb from limb, starting at your toes and fingers and working my way in to your torso. I'll make sure you don't miss a moment of it. And before you die, you'll see me holding your still beating heart before your open eyes. Do you hear me?"

She heard a coarse chuckle.

"Oh, I hear you loud and clear. I look forward to seeing you try."

Orin Rhodes abruptly ended the call.

Riley stepped on the accelerator. She knew she had no time to waste.

CHAPTER THIRTY SEVEN

Orin Rhodes took a ferocious swing at the bound man's face. He hit him so hard on the left cheek that his own fist hurt. The pain felt good. It was good to let off some steam. The truth was, Orin felt frustrated.

He'd just ended the call to Riley Paige, and he knew that she was on her way. But how long was it going to be before she got here? If she was still in Florida, her arrival could be hours away.

But how could he have found out her whereabouts? She'd never have told him over the phone. And to that extent, she had an advantage over him.

Not that it was much of an advantage. For the time being, he had absolute power over two lives that he knew she held dear. Still, he had to rein in his impulses. He wanted so much to shoot both father and daughter time and time again, relishing every moment of their pain. But he had to keep them alive for now.

He looked over at the daughter's face. With her mouth taped shut, she was staring at him and her father in stark terror. Her expression heartened him a bit. He wouldn't even have to hit *her* to cause her pain. All he had to do was keep right on tormenting her father.

The man's head had fallen forward, and he was whimpering softly through the tape on his mouth. Orin seized him by the hair and lifted up his face.

"Were you listening to that phone call?" he said in a sneering tone. "You didn't hear what your ex told me, did you? She told me to be her guest, and to beat you up to my heart's content."

With that lie, he drew back his fist, ready, and landed a blow to the man's chin.

He wondered how long he should keep him alive before killing him.

CHAPTER THIRTY EIGHT

Riley found the address and stopped the car outside the elegant vacation house. When she opened the car door, she noticed how quiet everything was. But as peaceful as the scene seemed to be, Riley knew that violence and terror hid just inside those walls.

She slipped out of the car and pushed the door shut as quietly as possible. She saw that lights were bright on the second floor, and she also saw some lights on in the third. The first floor was dark.

She wondered what was the best way to go in. Charging in through the main entrance wouldn't be smart. It would be better if she could get in unnoticed—if that was possible. She moved closer to the house to check for other options. She quickly found that a door to one side of the garage doors was standing ajar.

She felt a chill as she realized that this was where Rhodes himself had gotten in. Was he still there? If he was gone already, was anyone inside still alive?

She turned on her flashlight and walked into what appeared to be a storage room. She paused and listened carefully. She heard nothing. The whole house was absolutely still. That felt wrong to her—dreadfully, sickeningly wrong.

She opened the door at the opposite side of the room. Light poured in from above. Lying on the stairs nearby was a crumpled corpse that had tumbled down from a landing. Moving more closely, she saw that it was Darlene Olsen, the agent Lucy had sent to protect April and her father.

Riley felt a flash of guilt. She should have known that the young, green agent would have been no match for Orin Rhodes. And now all of her promise and potential had been cut brutally short.

But this was no time to fall into regret. Still keeping as quiet as possible, she made her way over and around the body and continued upward, step by careful step.

At the top of the stairs, she walked through an open door into a hallway. Lights were on everywhere. As she moved down the hall, she took quick glances into the kitchen and dining room as she passed them. She saw no one. With rising apprehension she crept toward double doors at the far end of the hallway.

When she stepped into the living room, she saw them—Ryan and April. They were both bound by duct tape to chairs in the middle of the room. Their mouths were taped shut. Ryan's head was bowed, but April was staring wild-eyed at her mother.

Riley rushed over to her daughter. As delicately as possible, she pulled the duct tape off her mouth. Riley was about to exclaim for joy when April interrupted her with a sharp whisper.

"Quiet! He's still in the house!"

Riley nodded with understanding. She saw Ryan's head was still bowed, and he seemed to be unconscious.

"How's your father?" Riley asked in a whisper.

"I dunno," April said. "He beat Daddy up pretty bad after he got us bound and gagged."

Riley stepped over to Ryan and leaned toward him. To her relief, she found that he still had a pulse and was breathing softly. Then Riley knelt down beside April.

"Where is he now?" she whispered.

"I dunno that either. He went out to the hallway. He hasn't come back since."

Riley stood up and listened. She couldn't hear anything. She walked back into the hallway, checking the kitchen and dining room again. Then she went back to the stairs. Looking around carefully, she spotted a thin trail of blood on the way up to the third floor.

The door at the top of the stairs opened into another hallway. The lights were on.

And there, to her complete shock, lay Orin Rhodes, lying on his side on the floor.

His wrists and ankles were hog-tied behind him with duct tape, and he was also gagged with the tape. A length of chain was wrapped around his neck. It rattled as he began to writhe in pain and terror. Riley could see that he'd been badly beaten, probably with the chain.

A butcher knife was lying nearby. But there was no blood on it, and Riley doubted that any of Orin's injuries had come from it.

At first, Riley couldn't process what had happened.

But then, staring at the battered killer, she began to realize.

Shane had been here.

He had distracted Rhodes from his prey and done this to him.

But was Hatcher still in the house?

Strangely, Riley found it hard to really care.

Just a little while ago she had vowed vengeance against Orin. And now he was lying helpless at her feet.

She picked up the knife, crouched down, and peered grimly into Orin Rhodes' eyes. She couldn't remember ever looking into the heart of such sheer terror. And he had good reason to be terrified.

Riley remembered the words she had said to him.

"Believe me, you've got no idea what the word pain *even means. You're going to find out, though."*

She felt her rage rising again—that bloodlust that she felt not only toward Rhodes, but all the monsters she had ever faced.

She could do it right now. She could hack Rhodes limb from limb. Perhaps she could even cut out his still-beating heart and show it to him before he died as she had threatened. She knew it wasn't impossible. Hundreds of years ago, executioners had routinely done that very thing in front of jeering crowds.

The thought was delicious. And the best part was that she could carry out her revenge with impunity. All she'd have to do was say that Hatcher had gotten here first and done it himself.

And who wouldn't believe her?

Why not? she thought.

She brandished the knife, looking for a place to make him hurt.

CHAPTER THIRTY NINE

With the knife in her hand, Riley hesitated. Something in Orin Rhodes' expression had changed.

She pulled the tape loose from his mouth. He gasped for air, then spoke.

"It's what he wants you to do, you know," Rhodes said. "It's why he left the knife here. He's testing you."

Riley realized that Rhodes was right. Hatcher meant this as a test of her character. And it had to do with that question he'd told her to ask herself.

"Am I already? Or am I becoming?"

Orin was smirking now. He didn't look scared anymore.

He doesn't think I'll go through with it, Riley thought.

The truth was, she was starting to have doubts herself.

"You'd better do it," he said. "Because if you don't, I swear to God, I'll get back at you. If it takes me the rest of my life, and if I have to escape from every prison on earth, I'll get my revenge. I'll make sure you suffer and then die."

Riley's fury was rising again. She gave Orin a sharp kick in the stomach. A groan burst out of his lungs. But then he laughed.

"Is that all you've got?" he said. "Because you told me you were going to teach me what pain means. And I barely felt that. You see, I've lived my life in pain. It's going to take a hell of a lot more than that to hurt me."

Riley savored his invitation.

She leaned back and kicked him hard across the face, so hard that he groaned for real this time as a tooth fell out.

His smirk was gone now.

She stood there, breathing hard, and didn't feel an ounce of pity or sympathy for him. She could easily imagine herself inflicting a slow, painful death on this animal, and never regretting it.

So why not? she asked herself again.

There was a good reason why not. She'd never be able to conceal what she'd done from Ryan and April. She knew they wouldn't contradict the lies she'd have to tell to get away with this. Nevertheless, they would also have to live with what she had done. They would be complicit. They didn't deserve that.

She set the knife aside. Still peering into Rhodes' eyes, she said, "Orin Rhodes, you are under arrest."

CHAPTER FORTY

Rhodes' expression changed from one of unspeakable horror to sheer perplexity.

Riley took out her cell phone and dialed 911.

"This is Riley Paige, FBI. I need police and paramedics. I'm bringing a dangerous criminal into custody. Another agent has been killed. The killer is injured, and so is another man."

The 911 operator dutifully took down the address.

Riley then hurried back down the stairs to help April and Ryan. But when she reached the landing, she saw a man standing at the bottom of the stairs.

It was Shane Hatcher, smiling up at her.

Instinctively, Riley drew her weapon and aimed it at him.

Hatcher held both hands out to his sides, palms facing her.

"I'm unarmed," he said. "What do you want to do?"

Riley stood there, paralyzed with indecision. It was her assignment to arrest him—or at least it had been until she'd been suspended. She could take him right now, alive or dead. In order to take him alive, she'd at least have to wound him. All she'd need to do was aim at his thigh and pull the trigger.

But she couldn't do it. Monster though he might be, he'd been a weird sort of ally. And if he hadn't stopped Rhodes just now, what might have become of April and Ryan?

"You've got questions you want to ask me," he said.

Riley nodded. Her head was buzzing with questions.

"Go ahead, ask them," Shane said.

"You've been on his trail all along," Riley said. "You could have killed him several times over. You could have killed him just now. Why didn't you do it?"

Hatcher shrugged.

"Why didn't *you* do it?" he said. "That's the real question, isn't it?"

Riley was trembling now, but she didn't know why.

"I didn't do it because I'm not like you," she said. "I'm not a monster."

Hatcher startled her with a burst of laughter.

"Oh, come on, Riley. Are you really going to try to tell me that you spared that bastard's life out of the goodness of your heart?"

The question brought Riley up short. She knew that he was absolutely right. The only reason she hadn't tortured and killed Orin Rhodes was out of concern for April and Ryan. She still more than half wished she could make him scream with pain.

Hatcher said, "Remember that question I told you to ask yourself? Are you already, or are you becoming? Well, I think you know the answer now. You're *becoming*. You're becoming what you've always been deep down. Call it a monster or whatever you want. And it won't be long before you *are* that person."

Riley wanted to tell him he was wrong. The words wouldn't come.

Hatcher's smile broadened.

"You owe me, Riley Paige," he said.

Then he turned slowly and disappeared down the stairs.

She knew she should chase him, apprehend him.

But she could not bring herself to.

And she did not know if she ever could.

And that, in some ways, scared her most of all.

*

Riley rushed back into the living room.

"Everything's going to be all right," she told April. "He can't hurt you."

Her hands were shaking as she tried to pull the tape that bound April.

"Check on Daddy first," April said.

Riley knew that April was right. She hurried over to Ryan and removed the gag from his mouth. To Riley's relief, he groaned softly. He was regaining consciousness.

She went back over to April and pulled the tape off of her. Unsteadily at first, April got up and helped Riley unbind Ryan. He was still barely conscious, so the two of them laid him out on the sofa.

By then, Riley could hear approaching ambulance sirens.

She also heard a clatter of footsteps coming up the stairs. Riley reflexively reached for her weapon. Then she breathed a huge sigh of relief as Bill burst into the room. As she'd expected, he'd found out where she was and had come to help. She hadn't thought he'd get here so fast.

"Are you OK?" Bill asked.

For some reason, Riley couldn't say a word. All she knew was that she didn't have to be strong—not anymore, not right now. She fell into Bill's arms and sobbed.

A few minutes later, Riley was standing beside an ambulance gurney watching a paramedic examine Ryan.

"How is he?" Riley asked.

176

"He's going to be all right," the paramedic said. "There's been some concussion, but I don't think his skull has been fractured. It could be a lot worse. My guess is he'll be out of the hospital in a few days."

Relieved, Riley took hold of Ryan's hand. He was still foggy and seemed to be having trouble focusing his eyes on her. He moved his mouth as if he wanted to say something to her. Riley bent closer to listen.

"Riley, I never knew," he whispered. "I never knew."

Before Riley could reply, the medical team lifted him into the ambulance.

Riley stood there, wondering what he'd meant. Was he trying to say that he had a new appreciation of the work Riley had to do in the world? Or was he trying to say that he had never comprehended the horror of her job until now?

She comforted herself with the thought that he wasn't badly hurt. And April seemed to be OK as well. The problem she faced right now was making things straight with her bosses in Quantico.

Will I ever be allowed to work again?

CHAPTER FORTY ONE

Riley gave her report at the meeting the next day in Quantico. She knew that the stakes were high. Carl Walder and Brent Meredith were both there. So were Bill, Emily Creighton, and Craig Huang.

Riley described the role that Shane Hatcher had played at Chincoteague—especially the way he had bound and gagged Orin Rhodes.

But she didn't relate what she and Hatcher had said to each other on the stairway. Riley was still haunted by what he'd told her.

"You're becoming what you've always been deep down. Call it a monster or whatever you want."

When Riley finished talking, everyone was silent for a moment.

"One thing seems certain," Brent Meredith said. "Hatcher was *not* Orin Rhodes' accomplice. Quite the opposite, in fact."

"Not so fast," Walder said with a growl. "Hatcher is still at large, and he's dangerous. He's killed one man already—the driver of the book truck at Sing Sing."

"I have reason to believe otherwise, sir," Riley said.

Walder gave her a baffled look.

"I have reason to believe that the driver was an accomplice in the escape," Riley continued. "I'm pretty sure that he was paid handsomely, and he's now out of the country."

Walder squinted at Riley.

"You have *reason to believe* all that?" he asked.

Another silence fell. Riley wondered if she was going to have to produce the photo Shane Hatcher had sent her of the driver relaxing on a beach.

Instead, Walder said, "Agent Paige, you consistently disobeyed my direct orders."

Riley gulped. Was she about to be fired?

Bill spoke up. "With all due respect, sir—would things have turned out better if Agent Paige *had* obeyed your orders?"

It was the perfect response, and Riley resisted the urge to smile. Walder had been consistently wrong all along. If she had followed his orders every step of the way, Rhodes would probably still be at large. Walder had no good answer to Bill's question.

"Agent Paige, I'm taking you off the Hatcher case," Walder said. "You're too close to it. Agents Creighton and Huang, you take over the hunt for Shane Hatcher."

Although Riley didn't say so, Walder's new orders suited her fine. He was right—she really was too close to Hatcher. She wasn't even sure her heart was fully into trying to capture him. Besides, it was an impossible task. Shane, she knew, would not be found unless he wanted to be. On his terms. Creighton and Huang, of all people, hadn't a chance in the world.

"What do you want me to do, sir?" Riley asked.

Walder drummed his fingers on the table for a moment.

"Await further orders," he finally said. "I'm sure you'll be needed on another case soon."

Then to the whole group, Walder said, "That will be all for today. Thank you all for the good work."

As the meeting broke up, Riley exchanged glancing smiles with both Bill and Meredith. They looked as relieved as she was that she still had a job.

More than that, they seemed proud of her. Once again, she had managed to achieve what all the other agents couldn't.

And despite all the nonsense, all the internal politics, that silent look of approval, from people she truly respected, sustained her.

CHAPTER FORTY TWO

The next night, at home in their townhouse, Riley and April huddled together on the couch. They were gobbling popcorn and watching the most trivial programs they could find on TV.

Riley was amazed by April's strength and resilience. She had some bruises from her ordeal, but showed little or no emotional trauma. She'd come through this experience stronger than she had been before. Somehow, beating Rhodes on his first attack had given her greater confidence.

Riley was more worried about Ryan. He was in the hospital now, recovering from a concussion. He was going to be all right, but he'd definitely been traumatized.

Riley remembered what he'd said to her.

"Riley, I never knew. I never knew."

Riley still wasn't sure what he'd meant. And she had no idea what their relationship would be like now. Was there any way of bringing back the small bit of trust they were starting to feel together? And what about Blaine? He, too, had been traumatized and nearly killed.

She remembered what Blaine had said to her in the hospital.

"There isn't much I wouldn't do for you and April."

How far did Blaine mean that, really? Would he have second thoughts about getting close to her? She couldn't blame him if he did.

All Riley knew for sure was that she felt terrible about putting two of the most important men in her life in such danger. Bill was able to deal with the risks that came with the job. She couldn't expect the same from Ryan and Blaine.

Another thought was lurking in her mind, making her feel sad.

April seemed to pick up on her mother's melancholy.

"What's wrong, Mom?" she asked, snuggling close.

Riley sighed, trying to think of how to put it into words. She had recently told April all about what had happened in New York sixteen years ago. Maybe now April could help her come to terms with it.

"I keep thinking about Heidi—Orin Rhodes' girlfriend."

"It wasn't your fault, Mom," April said.

"Wasn't it?" Riley said. "When I killed her, I set Orin Rhodes on a long, twisted path. And now four more people are dead."

April pulled out of their embrace and looked her in the eye.

"Mom, think about it. If you hadn't killed her and arrested him, they would have kept right on killing. Believe me, I know. I got a real taste for how cruel he could be. Who knows how many more people would have died?"

Riley didn't reply. She tried to let April's words sink in.

"Besides," April said, "if you hadn't killed Heidi, she'd have killed you. Then I wouldn't have been born. Believe me, I really don't like that idea."

Riley smiled. "Well, maybe you would have been born—only with a different mother."

April shook her head.

"You mean I'd have wound up with one of Daddy's bimbo socialites for a mom? Huh-uh. If you think I've been rebellious in *this* life, it's nothing compared to what I'd have been like if things had gone that way."

Riley chuckled a little, and so did April.

Riley realized that April was right in a way. The strong young woman sitting here beside her had actually benefitted from the clash of values between herself and Ryan. April was learning to make choices, not just accept whatever seemed cool. And she was learning to take care of herself.

*

Riley had just relaxed again and was trying to focus on some silly TV show when the phone rang.

It was Garrett Holbrook, her FBI colleague in Arizona, the one who had found a home for Jilly with his sister, Bonnie Flaxman. Riley's heart sank as she prepared for bad news.

"Riley, I'm afraid Jilly has run away again," Garrett said.

"Why?" Riley asked. "What happened?"

"Bonnie and her husband found out that Jilly had been going back to the truck stop where you first found her."

Riley's despair deepened. She had rescued Jilly at a truck stop when she was just getting ready to try her hand at prostitution. Riley could hardly believe that Jilly had revisited that awful world.

"Bonnie and her husband went and found her, then grounded her," Garrett said. "She didn't take it well, and a day later she was gone."

Riley didn't know what to say.

"Riley, Bonnie says she can't deal with this anymore. She was hoping to adopt her, but this whole thing has shocked her out of that idea. Jilly said she just wanted to visit friends, but Bonnie's afraid that Jilly's going to wind up a prostitute after all. I've been trying to find her to take her back to the shelter. So far I've had no luck."

Riley drew a deep breath. Her mood sank again.

"Thanks for letting me know, Garrett. Please tell me if—*when* you find her."

"I will."

Riley hung up and sat there staring at the muted TV.

April said, "It's about Jilly, isn't it? She's run away again?"

Riley nodded.

"What are you going to do?" April asked.

The question hung heavily in the air, as Riley realized she had no idea.

"Are you just going to leave her all alone and lost like that?" April finally asked.

Riley was taken aback by the depth of April's concern.

"Jilly needs help," Riley said. "But what can I do for her? Everybody around me gets hurt sooner or later. Besides, the world is full of problems. I can't solve all of them."

"No," April said. "You can't. But you can solve one of them. And for that one person, that's the whole world, isn't it?"

Riley stared back at her daughter, in awe of her wisdom, truly floored and impressed by her. Beyond that, touched.

Riley couldn't help but nod back.

"I can help," April said softly, holding her hand. "You bring her back here, and I can help raise her." April looked up at her with pleading, desperate eyes. "I *need* to help," she added.

Riley knew in that moment that her daughter was talking about herself; she saw herself in Jilly, and it would be somehow cathartic for her to rescue her.

Riley sighed, feeling the weight of the world on her shoulders.

"I don't know, April," she said. "I just don't know."

*

Later that night, long after April had fallen asleep, Riley sat up in her bed, unable to sleep. She checked the clock: two a.m.

She got up and quietly paced the quiet house, all still except for her. April's words still rang in her head:

For that one person, that's the whole world, isn't it?

And:

I need to help.

Riley dwelled on it.

And the more she did, the more she realized that she needed to help, too.

There was a young girl out there who needed her, who had no one else in the world to turn to.

And if Riley turned her back on her, it would be as good as letting her die.

Riley took a deep breath, and she knew what she had to do.

She would go to Arizona.

And bring Jilly back.

COMING SOON!

Book #6 in the Riley Paige mystery series!

BOOKS BY BLAKE PIERCE

RILEY PAIGE MYSTERY SERIES
ONCE GONE (Book #1)
ONCE TAKEN (Book #2)
ONCE CRAVED (Book #3)
ONCE LURED (Book #4)
ONCE HUNTED (Book #5)
ONCE PINED (Book #6)

MACKENZIE WHITE MYSTERY SERIES
BEFORE HE KILLS (Book #1)
BEFORE HE SEES (Book #2)
BEFORE HE COVETS (Book #3)

AVERY BLACK MYSTERY SERIES
CAUSE TO KILL (Book #1)
CAUSE TO RUN (Book #2)

Blake Pierce

Blake Pierce is author of the bestselling RILEY PAGE mystery series, which include the mystery suspense thrillers ONCE GONE (book #1), ONCE TAKEN (book #2), ONCE CRAVED (#3) and ONCE LURED (#4). ONCE HUNTED (#5), and ONCE PINED (#6). Blake Pierce is also the author of the MACKENZIE WHITE mystery series and AVERY BLACK mystery series.

An avid reader and lifelong fan of the mystery and thriller genres, Blake loves to hear from you, so please feel free to visit www.blakepierceauthor.com to learn more and stay in touch.

Made in the USA
Middletown, DE
24 August 2018